TWISTED
LIFE

TIME SLIPS, REALITY SHIFTS & ALIENS

PAUL IESON

Angry Eagle Publishing
Htps://AngryEaglePublishing.com

Dedication

For Willow

CONTENTS

Introduction

NOTE The first two chapters of the story Twisted Life will read more as an outline but will get juicy fast enough with a good story line. The story is written in story teller fashion for a reason. It is to make you, the reader, feel like you are sitting around a firepit being told a story from a first hand account.

Paul leson

Chapter One

I haven't had a fire out back in weeks. It's a nice day and there is a nice change from the amount of wind we have had this summer. So I'm going to get the firepit ready for tonight when the rest of my friends get here. Tonight is supposed to be pretty decent, as in not too cold or hot, so people will be able to enjoy the evening.

I get about halfway through setting things up when I have to stop and take a phone call. It's my granddaughter calling me from the house. She's letting me know I have an unexpected visitor in the driveway. One thing I can say about this day and age we live in, cellphones can be so convenient.

I ask her to send whomever it is to the back where I am. I will deal with them here. My granddaughter does just that. I am confronted by someone I have not seen in twenty five years. This meeting has just thrown me for a loop. I stop dead with everything I am doing and look in disbelief.

It's my second stepfather, William. I have not seen this man in twenty five years, and he can only be here for one reason. My mother has to be dead. I can think of nothing else that would bring him here and no, I am not happy about this.

"Well, hello there, William. How did you even know where I live and to what do I owe this unexpected visit?" I am attempting to be as pleasant as I possibly can. "Please, have a seat."

William takes a seat and says, "Thank you". I offer him a glass of scotch and take a seat next to him.

"Well?" I have the firepit set up enough that I light the fire in an attempt to take up some of the unpleasant silence. Then I give my full attention to my visitor.

After I sit back and light a cigar, I speak again. "You don't have to say a word my friend. I already know. Your wife, Cindy, is dead."

It takes a few minutes for him to speak but he begins to talk. "I find it amazing that you already know this. I suppose I didn't need to drive all the way out here then, did I?"

"Oh, I think you came out here for more than to simply tell me your wife is dead."

Will finishes his glass of scotch. "You are correct about that. More scotch, please?"

"Help yourself." I get up and add more wood to the fire, then look around to see if anyone else is here yet. "So, exactly why are you here? If I can ask."

"Your mother told me all sorts of things. A lot of them are very hard for me to believe but she is, was, my wife and I love her, so I never called her on her story. I just listened to what she told me. The funny thing about it is her sister tells me that it is all true and so does her husband."

I sit in my chair for a few minutes without saying a word. I am thinking to myself and trying to decide how I want to go about telling this man the story of my life and how my mother fits into it all. So, I take a few more drags off of my cigar, then stand up to play with the fire again. Finally, I make the decision to just tell him.

"Fine, William. I will tell you the complete story and hold nothing out of it. I tell you now that everything I say will be the truth. I don't care how far out it sounds. But I ask you one thing and that is I do not want you to interrupt me unless you need something. Agreed?"

"Yes. I really want to hear this. I have been wondering about it now for days." I can tell he is sincere but just as I am to begin this story, I see someone else walking towards the firepit.

It is my longtime friend, River. This is cool because she is actually a big part of this story, and I am happy she is here. She walks up to me, kisses me on the cheek, then says, "Hello, sweetie." She takes a seat looking at me like "Who is this guy sitting here?"

"This, River dear, is my second stepfather, William. Cindy is dead, finally."

"What a shame." I could hear the sarcasm in her voice. "And why is he here?" River can be rude sometimes, but she doesn't mean to be.

"I was about to tell him our story. My mother told him her version of things, so I am telling him the way it was." I add more wood to the fire. Then grab a staff out of the woodpile so I have something to play with while I talk. Then I begin:

My grandparents were off-worlders. They came from another world far from here. My mother and her sister are the same. I will not tell the name of the planet they come from but I will say that THEY, as in their kind, have been here for a long time. Their species are responsible for reseeding the planet twice after the two great extinction events on this world. However, my father is human. So, this makes me a half breed, or whatever. Hell, I don't know. What I do know is that I have never fit in anywhere and when I try, things just go to hell.

First memory: I do remember being inside the womb just before birth. I know no one else ever does, but I do. I can remember not wanting to be here and I also remember this bright ass light in my eyes, but I could not see where the light was coming from. Then I could hear the muffled sounds of people talking. It was like trying to hear what is said behind a wall in another room. I was fighting to stay where I was because I knew what was about to happen and I did not want to go through that shit again.

I cannot stop moving out and into the world we are now all stuck in, though. I can hear the woman known in this world as my mother, screaming at the nurse to make sure that she circumcises my ass and that she should take as much skin as she can. I start screaming.

William speaks up and I can tell he already does not want to hear what I have to say. "I am sorry, but I have to call bullshit. No one ever remembers being born."

"Will, I can stop right fucking now. I do remember it and I said no interruptions. So do I continue?" I glare at him, awaiting a response.

"Okay, sorry. Please go on. I will shut up." He has a sarcastic look about him.

"Fine..."

Next memory: My best guess is that I am about 6 months old. I am laying in my playpen and listening to music. I am having a conversation with someone I know in my head. He tells me I am a boy and I argue with him that I'm not. I was supposed to be a chick this time. Then he tells me to look down at myself and I do. I am a boy. I start yelling, "Arron! Arron!" That is my mother's name on the other side. She hears me telepathically. Something she says she could only do with me and my sister, but I know better.

She walks over to me and says to me, "My name is not Arron. It is Cindy now. Your father should be home soon, so I need to shut this off. He does not like me listening to this music." So, she walks over to one of those old ass radio consoles. To my surprise the song playing is Go Ask Alice by Jefferson Airplane. Now get this shit. It is 1963. This song was not recorded until 1969. So anyway, she takes the record off the turntable, grabs the record cover and puts it inside the radio.

She comes back over to me. "Do not think that I don't know who you are and that I forgot what you did. You are mine now and I will make your life a living hell for as long as I can. Everything that you say, I will tell people is a lie. I don't care what it is. Every time something happens, you did it. I am the adult and you are the child, so people will believe me and not you." I remember nothing else from that moment. I will add here that this would mean that I had already been through all this before, but at this point I do not remember much of anything.

Memory three: Myself and my mother were driving through the country, going I have no clue where. I think it was home since we lived out in the country. We were in a station wagon and I was in the back. It was the 60s. No one cared about safety back then. It was raining and we were at a stop sign. I noticed a carnival truck off on the side of the road, right across the street from us. I saw what looked like guys dressed as clowns walking towards us in the rain and was screaming at my mother that she needed to step on the gas and get out of here before they got to us. She was looking but did not see what I was talking about. I was yelling, "Can't you see? It's the Aliens and they are here to get me." I remember they got to the car then nothing else but waking up at home. This was the first encounter with the grays that I can remember.

What I was to learn later is that they took me right out of the car that time. My mother drove home and when she got there I was nowhere to be found. She looked frantically for me because my dad was about to get home and she didn't want to get her ass beat. She found me on my bed asleep, a place she had already checked multiple times. She never told my father of this incident as far as I know.

Then at age five, we moved into town and my sister was born. I was abruptly told that I was not allowed to hold her, ever, because she knew that if I did, I would drop her on her head and kill her. This is the sort of thing I had to deal with at five.

At, let's say nine or ten, we were waiting for my dad who was in the town bar with someone named Tigger. When I say we I mean my mother, me and my sister. Again, just wait.

It was at this age that I wanted to learn to play guitar. I did end up getting one at Christmas time. I was so happy until I realized that this was not the guitar I was wanting, so I put it down for many years. I wanted it because I had memories of playing the guitar and I thought that I could just pick it up and start playing. That was not the case. It would be a few years before I realized that I would have to learn all over again.

"At ten I was standing at the front door looking out with my dad standing next to me. "Why is mom getting on that motorcycle with the neighbor kid?" My dad replies, "Because she used to ride with Tigger, and she misses it. So, I said she could. She told me how she used to love riding with you on your bike and how she knows you are Tigger. He, is you? Right?"

I was at a loss for words and did not know what to say so I did not say a lot. "I know about Tigger, but I am not Tigger."

We just stood at the screen door and watched my mother ride off.

Paul Ieson

I refused to admit that I was Tigger to anyone for about 20 years.

On September 8th, 1974, the famous daredevil Evel Knievel climbed into a rocket and attempted to blast across the Snake River Canyon. My little sister, my dad and I were all in the living room watching it on TV. However, my mother would not come in the room and refused to watch. When we asked why, all she would say is that is when the incident occurred. This will make more sense later.

However, between you and me, I already knew what she was talking about. She had something to do with a time traveler in her teens. Supposedly, this time traveler was me and she was hurt the last time she went anywhere with me, badly, and that was why she did not want to watch. She said she was not going to relive the incident again. This incident is also why she treats me like shit.

In '75 my dad died. I was twelve at the time and this is how it went down. My parents had a boat and school was just over. We were out on the river and my dad asked my mom for something to drink. I watched my mother pour my dad's bottle of nitroglycerin pills into his glass of soda. My dad had a heart problem. She had my sister take the soda to him at the same time he was on the radio with his friends on the Harbor Patrol. He took a few sips of his drink and fell over on the windowsill of the boat. At twelve I did not understand what was going on 'til after the fact. He died, and because the police witnessed this part of the event, they said it was a heart attack. There was no autopsy. My mother had just gotten away with murder.

Just after the funeral, I was sent away for about two weeks to stay with my best friend who had moved away. I forgot everything I had witnessed until much later in life which was the intention of sending me away. I had a lot of mixed emotions about this since he was sitting right next to me when he went to the other side. Also, I was happy I would not have to put up with his strict ass any more. I did not know that things were about to change for the worse and throw me for a loop.

Six months later. My mother was secretly starting to go out with my dad's best friend, David, who lived right down the street from us. They were married inside of a year. In my mind it was confirmation to me that my mother did not love my father. It was also around this time I started to become my own person. I also started to remember who I was and why I was here on this shit hole planet again. I had a lot of unfinished crap that needed to be taken care of.

"Will, you were David's best friend, weren't you? It seems to be a pattern with my mother." He just glares at me but says nothing.

Anyway, I was a typical teen-aged kid. However, my life was anything but typical. I grew up in children's homes. One home was the doing of my parents. One was my doing. I could not take the abusive crap so I checked myself into a home and they kept me after learning what I had gone through.

Ready for this shit? After my mother remarried, my stepfather insisted that we all go to this new church and we did. I did not have a say even though everyone in the family knew I did not believe in God and wanted to stay home.

When I was thirteen, my stepfather and the reverend from this church said they wanted to take me to an old airport to watch the remote-controlled planes and stuff that they knew I was into. It was supposed to bring me closer to the adults, they said. A sort of bonding moment, if you will. We never made it to the airport. Instead of going to do this thing that was planned, all three of us ended up at this cheap motel. I will not go into details about what happened, but they both had their way with me sexually.

Later I found out my mother knew where we were going and what happened but did not care. When I tried to bring it up to her, she called me a liar. Then things got really bad for me. Though the sex thing never happened again, I was denied food and sleep and forced to stay in my room. It was that way from then on out. I was never allowed to leave the house alone, either, with the only exception of school. In my later years, I could not even have a friend or girlfriend call on the phone or visit the house without my mother calling them every name in the book. They made sure I was alone. Now you understand why I left and checked into a children's home.

I did have a few girlfriends in high school. The problem was I could only have anything to do with them while I was in school. So we would skip classes and do stuff then. Needless to say, this was not enough for the girls and we would break up over it every time.

Not to get sidetracked, but I do need to tell you a few things about the children's home in Maumee. I was happy when that place closed down. There was so much going on there to hurt kids. The place closing down meant that would stop. However, I will tell you about the home at the end of my story, not now. I don't need you to be confused.

I graduated high school in '81. I got no graduation party or "I am proud of you" or anything like that. I got two bags of groceries and the first month's rent paid on a room. I was told to get the fuck out. This, I gladly did, but it took me a while to understand why the bullshit did not stop.

As it turns out, my mother would call me, acting like she was concerned about me, and I would tell her that I found a new job or whatever. The next day, I would be fired for no reason. After I figured out what was going on, I never told her where I was working, or much of anything for that matter, because she would get me fired every time I did tell her. Oh, and to top it all off, I ended up being diagnosed with epilepsy. My mother did not believe anything was wrong with me. She said I was just trying to get attention. Then, a few years later when I was in front of a judge for a speeding ticket and had a seizure, she had no choice but to acknowledge what was going on with me. That was some bullshit, if you ask me.

Oh, and the alien thing? It kept on happening throughout my childhood years. They would just come and take me to their ship and I would be missing for a few days. My mother and stepfather, and also my dad knew when he was alive, knew what was going on. They knew what was going on but they knew they couldn't do a thing about it so life just went on. They would just lie about where I was or say I was sick or whatever. In those days, no one checked up on stuff like that. It was not like it is today.

I should also tell you about the friend I talked to in my head a lot from when I was younger and all the way through my 20s. To this day, I do not know who he really was, but he would help me when I got into trouble and guided me through stuff. However, if I listened to him at other times, he would end up getting me into trouble. He also was the one who talked me into getting into the occult.

That was just a glimpse into my childhood and since I do not wish to bore you, I will stop here. Now a fast run down of the next 20 years.

My first few months of being 18 were wonderful for me. Freedom! I got a job at a record store and met a girl who I considered a girlfriend named Brandy but she thought I was more of a friend-with-benefits thing. I had trouble with that but it was only because I had never experienced anything like it before. Needless to say, it didn't last long because I was an idiot.

In the spring of when I was 18, I went to Florida. I hitch hiked the entire way there. My life was shit and I wanted a change. I had lost a very cool job and my place to live and, at the very least, I wanted to be picked up by someone who would end up killing my ass since I was unable to do it myself for more reasons than you might think.

When I came back to the suburbs of Toledo, I met my first girlfriend, who really was a girlfriend I actually got to have regular sex with. We were only together for a little over two or three years. May have been longer, I don't remember, but in this time we had twin girls and, from what I understand, later a boy.

The girls were one year and ten days old. Cindy, my girlfriend slash wife or whatever the hell she was to me that day, decided to leave and go to her brother's. I was told she would be back. Well, she didn't come back so I walked to her brother's house five miles away and asked what was up. She told me to get out and that we were done with our relationship. So I left but I only took the clothes on my back so I would have the excuse to come back later. Unbeknownst to me, she went back home that night.

I ended up spending the night at my friend's house and in the morning, we all were woken up by the sound of Cindy beating down the door. I went out of the trailer to find out what was wrong with her. All the neighbors that were up at this time of the morning could hear me go off, yelling, "Just what the hell is your problem? I thought you wanted me gone."

Cindy replied in a pissed off voice, "Tricia is dead and it's all your fault!" Tricia was the younger twin.

This took me off guard. I mean what a fucking way to be told your child is dead. "Just what the fuck are you talking about? Are you high? I think you are lying to me just to fuck with me." She said no, that she wasn't lying. I said I didn't believe her and told her to fuck off and went back inside. I called my mother. She would know the truth and, for once, I thought she would tell it. And she did. Yes, my child was indeed dead. I was devastated.

My friends asked me what that was all about and I told them. Of course, they did not know how to act after being told something like this. So they just said they would give me some time to digest all this and they walked into the other room. All this was very hard to wrap my head around. All I had was guilt in my head. I should not have left the house. I should have been there for the kids. I was so depressed I could not get off the couch all that day.

I won't go through it all here but this is what happened. You can't make this shit up. Cindy told everyone, the cops, EMTs, I mean everyone, that Tricia was asleep and somehow, while sleeping, the child had gotten her head stuck between the crib slats. This worked for her until the autopsy was done. The autopsy said something altogether different. Then the TV show 60 Minutes got their hands on the story as well since it went nationwide. Cindy kept to her story even though everyone by then knew she was a lying bitch.

Where was I through all this crap? I was living in my own misery. I knew nothing about the show on TV until after it aired. The other weird thing in all this, not one damn time did any cop, or anyone else, ever talk to me. It was like I did not exist and during this time I did not care. I just wanted to die. I never did see my other children again. Cindy had the male child while she was in prison. I wonder about him to this day.

What ended up really happening to Tricia was that she died of shaken baby syndrome. Cindy got five to twenty-five years for involuntary manslaughter but only served five months before getting out on shock probation. What the hell is shock probation? I ended up talking to shrinks who did nothing for me and I ended up on the street until I was able to pull my head out of my ass enough to get an income and my own place again.

In that day and age, when you had something like epilepsy, no one wanted to hire you. So, I washed dishes for $3.25 an hour and found a small place for one hundred bucks a month. This was all back in '85, by the way. I was also seeing a shrink and hanging out at this place for mental people on my off hours. Or I was getting stoned a lot. I still wanted to die, but I trucked on and got married to some flaked out chick. It was the thing to do at the time but did not last long. She did help me to apply for SSI so I could get medical and some sort of income. Alas, I was denied and ended up back on the street. So before I split town and went back to Florida I reapplied for disability.

It was the beginning of 1986 and I was in Florida. It was a cold ass night for being in LakeLand, the night before they launched the space shuttle, and I heard that ever familiar voice in my head. He told me that the shuttle would explode just after launch, and everyone would die. Then he told me that I could do something about it. We argued for a while because I knew damn well there was nothing I could do about it. I told him to just let things happen the way they did last time to shut him up. Then he was gone. We all know what happened that next day... a very sad day it was for everyone.

I stuck around in Florida for another month before I decided to head back to Toledo. When I did leave, things would forever change for me again. I had no means of transportation so I hitchhiked. Hoping to die. Needless to say, that didn't happen and every time it seems like it might, something stops it but I haven't figured out why yet.

First, I ended up spending sixteen hours in the Atlanta airport because the city was shut down over snow, of all things. This sucked badly because it took four days to get that far and I was starving. I ended up taking shelter inside the Atlanta airport and got to meet a guy who built coffins. I never did get anything to eat and I was famished.

Then it seemed my luck had changed a bit because I found a ride with this old guy who was going all the way to Ohio. Keep in mind that since I was not in the right frame of mind, I had forgotten that it was still winter and didn't even own a coat. We had a good time driving back to Ohio. Sometimes I would drive while he slept and vice versa. It worked well till the last time that I went to sleep. He was supposed to let me out of the car when we got to Cincinnati so I could take 75 the rest of the way but he didn't. He let me sleep and I woke up in Columbus. I was pissed. I had no coat and my dumb ass had to get out and try to get a ride in a foot of blowing snow.

I ended up walking through Worthington, Ohio because no one would give me a ride. When I finally got one, he said he was going to Toledo but he lied and dropped me into a raging snow storm in the middle of no-fucking-where. He must have thought he was being funny or something.

Now keep in mind, this is a snow storm. I have a tee-shirt and a windbreaker on, jeans and tennis shoes. That is it and I thought that this was the end. Finally, after all the times I thought in my life that I would die, this was going to be the end. There was no way it was not going to happen. It was not the way I would want to go, freezing to death, but it seemed this was what was going to happen. This next part is a bit unbelievable, but I swear on all that is good that this really happened.

I started screaming at the top of my lungs that I knew I was going to die and there was nothing anyone was going to do about it, including the aliens. I went on for a few minutes, but all I could hear was the sound of the wind. I was getting ready to just fall out into a snow drift and let myself die when I heard the voice of my old friend in my head telling me to relax, that there was someone that wanted to speak to me.

It was the aliens. They told me I didn't have to die, that I had the ability to go home from where I was, just like that. I told them to leave me alone and that I just wanted to die. They told me they could not allow that to happen and that I had too much that I had to do, that I had to go back in time and take care of unfinished business and other crap like that. Then they proceeded to tell me how to jump from one location to another.

I told them off. I remember getting ready to just fall out onto the ground and give up but I ended up a half block away from a homeless shelter in Toledo and it was dark. To this day I do not know if I did this or if they did, but there I was, cold and tired. As I was walking over to the shelter, there was a friend of mine by the door and he told me that my wife was looking for me. She had a place for me to stay and that I had also gotten my SSI. I decided that it was time to pull myself together and have a real life instead of living in shit.

Often, from this point on, I wondered if I was still in the snow drift and all this was playing out in my head before I finally died, that life from this moment on was just an illusion. How else could I explain time travel, among other shit?

Chapter Two

t took me a while, but I did end up getting my shit together. I had a nice apartment and went back to school. I took electronics and got an associate's degree. I was feeling pretty good about this, too. But even through all the faking myself through life, I still wanted out. I wanted to die. Everything just seemed so damn pointless.

My epilepsy was still a pain in my ass and holding me back. I had one doctor that wanted me to wear a damn helmet, another wanting to cut my head open and so on. So, I turned in another direction.

I had remembered what my friend had said about the occult and so not knowing any better, I tried to contact someone that did not exist. However, another did answer and things were starting to go in my favor for a change.

I did not realize at the time it was the aliens pretending to be a god. They took my epilepsy away. Though things like this are best kept secret, I will tell you the outcome. Life got better. My epilepsy was gone and I finally had gotten into a good spot in life. I met a girl that I ended up living with. She was about five years older than me and had three kids. This relationship lasted about 10 years and I thought this girl would be the love of my life. Until we parted ways, both agreeing it would be best because we were no longer compatible. She had turned born again Christian and I could not deal with that. When we parted, it messed me up pretty bad for a few years until I could get over myself.

How did I get over myself? The occult. I was at wit's end in life once again. Though I won't go into detail, I will tell you that the occult allowed me to become a better person. It taught me how to take responsibility for myself and how things were no one's fault but mine because everything in my life is my doing. I was now a Pagan and learning how to make things go my way for a change. To hell with what people said about how life was supposed to go.

I got myself a job with the railroad and life was good until I lost my job and it was time to take responsibility for that. I had fucked my life up, not anyone else, and the only one I could blame was me.

Now I was living with a few friends in the same apartment because it was cheaper that way. All I had in life were my clothes and a few other things including my motorcycle. It seemed to keep coming back to me even though I would sell it when times got too hard. We all are into the cult movie thing and life was what it was.

Then me and my friend River shared living space. We started talking one day and told each other how we knew one another, even though, in this reality, it was the first time we were in each other's lives. We finished each other's stories about the memories that we had about our lives together, things we clearly remember doing, but in this life, had not done yet. Like me playing music for a living and River singing the songs.

River was this scrawny redhead who had the temper to go along with her hair. She was about 5 foot 6 and if she turned sideways and stuck out her tongue she would look like a zipper. She liked to live the Gothic lifestyle and she was a free spirit. We were close but in a friend only sort of way.

I forgot to tell you about me at this time. I was six feet tall. I wore mostly black, had long hair and was never seen without my leather jacket or trench on. I rode a 750 Yamaha because it was so much cheaper to own than a car. This was where life got interesting for me.

I also have to add that everything I am about to tell you is the truth. Whether you want to believe it or not, it did happen. This is the first time I am telling this story to anyone. I tell this to piss off the fucking praying mantis-looking bastard aliens that think they can just fuck with some one's life like it's okay.

Here comes the big twist. Before I get any further into this story that I am telling you, I think I should explain a few things you should know before you think I am entirely full of shit. As you know, I am half human and half something else. I immediately drew the attention of that damned insect species and have been abducted since birth by their gray drones. They decided to give me this ability to go back and forth through time. They turned me into a damn experiment. They wanted to see exactly how time could be manipulated since time seems to be valid only on this planet we all reside on. It took me a long time to understand what and why they did this and so I made a few rules to go by that I would end up breaking more than once.

The aliens are the entire reason I got myself into the occult. It was to find a way to keep the aliens away from me and it worked. Using magic, I disabled the damn tracking implants that always seemed to move when I tried to cut them out. I made myself invisible to them. However, every once in a while, they would still find me and take me.

I am a high priest in the occult. A reiki master and healer. I am also a time traveler. At this point in my life, I was around thirty-five. Or I should say I looked thirty-five and told people I was thirty five. Remember what I told you about the snowstorm and how I should have died but didn't. I have been abducted throughout my life and the ability of my time travel and reality slipping is the aliens' doing. It's like I am a fucking lab rat.

During the time that I was living at River's, I went to places like the war of 1812 but I was there in 1811. Since I spent several months there, the commodore was a good friend of mine. Tesla and Einstein were good friends, as well. As it would turn out, I learned a great deal from everyone I would go to visit and become friends with. However, learning to keep my mouth shut about things was a challenge at first but I had no choice but to do so. I might add that I was with Tesla the day he died. He gave me all the work that he had in his room. So, it was not the government that took his work, it was me. I did it and this is one of the reasons that THEY, the government, want my ass.

I was there on April 14, 1865, when Lincoln was shot. I should say here that I had met the man a few times and he knew me well. You will never read about this in the history books, though, because it was kept quiet. Anyway, about a half hour before Lincoln was shot, I met him at one of the theater doors and finally agreed to take him to my time. I saw no problem with this since he would be shot soon. So I brought him to 2010, where he was very disappointed with things in our time. He did not care for many things, like the smell and the fact that it was too loud, as far as he was concerned, and all the rudeness. When we got back, I was a few minutes late. I wanted to tell him not to go to his box alone, but kept my mouth shut and bid him a good night. It was hard to let him die but what could I do?

Tesla was a weird one. He only cared for enough to survive. He was a very open man and would tell you anything you wanted to know and if you were not careful, he would show you whatever it was he was working on at the time. It did not matter if you understood it or not. It was the alien thing that we had in common because he had been abducted, too. It was sad when he died. No one wanted a thing to do with him so he spent his time talking to himself, the four walls and a bird.

Then there was Commodore Perry. He was a good friend. I cannot tell you how many nights we spent around the fire, smoking cigars and drinking scotch. He did get quite upset with me once for cussing in front of his wife but other than that, it was a real nice time I spent with him by Lake Erie. Lastly, he was the one who taught me how to shoot and he even gave me a set of dueling pistols I wish I still had.

In the 1980s, that was going back in time, too. At this point, I was working with a scientist and we worked for the government. By 1990, a secret power plant had been built for research of perpetual motion. The power plant worked, but the government had it shut down fast as it was working on its own and producing power. The government had one main scientist killed and they tried to kill my friend. They did something even worse to him. They took it all away. They took his degrees all the way back through high school and to top it all off, he could not work even if he had wanted to because he had lost the use of his hands. Me? I got out of there before anyone could get me. THEY did not know who I was at this point.

I will add this now. If you're back in time and step on a butterfly, it changes nothing at all. Teaching small things to ordinary people does nothing to change history, at all. While I was in 1811, had I told a slave that in 1863 they would have their freedom, for example, it would have really messed up the timeline. Had I given Tesla the secret to perpetual motion, I would have messed things up then, as well. See where I am going with this? If I play a country song on my guitar from my time, it changes nothing. But if I claimed that same song as mine and it became a hit? Well, I think you can see where I am going with this.

I got tired of doing this stuff after a while, so I decided I wanted to take the slow path for a while in the time I was in. I needed a break. Some things I just did not want to live without. Like toilet paper, running water and a hot shower. Also, the fact that it would take days to go fifty miles a hundred years ago, and it can be done in this time in forty five minutes. This was also when I got stupid.

I would take people back in time with me on my motorcycle just to prove to them I could do it. I was tired of people thinking I was a nutcase and not believing me. So, I would do things like go back and take a photo with whoever I was with at the time. Then go back to the present day and show people where I had been. One time, I took a pic and so had the local newspaper. Back in 1906, I think it was. When we got back to the present time, I was stupid enough to show the news people and that was a big mistake. The news had a field day with it and everyone said it was fake. I should have just stopped right then and left. Then people would have forgotten all about it but I didn't and it made life hard for a while.

Then I met this lady, I'll call her Lynn. She had a couple of kids and was divorced. I ended up spending a lot of time with her family but I did not live with her. We might as well have been living together as much as I was there. We did everything together and when her first granddaughter was born, I helped to take care of the child because, well, I won't go into that.

After about 10 years or so we moved out into the country. She had her house and I got something down the street from her. I am still spending a lot of time at Lynn's place so I would help with doing the stuff around the house that Lynn could not do because she had no time. She had to work. In return I could use her shed to work on my projects. I would work on free energy stuff. I built a generator and hooked it to her house. Mistake.

I made the error of unhooking the house from the power company. They came out to the house to see what was going on and told me to unhook my generator, that I was in trouble for messing with their stuff. Right after they left, four guys in black suits showed up. They looked at my generator and then took it, not saying a word until they were ready to leave. All they said was, "Try anything like this again and it is prison for you. I should just stop it all if I were you. We know who you are and we will find you wherever you go. This is your only warning."

To say the least, I was pissed. It did confirm one thing to me. Parts of the government knew more than they told the public and kept a tight lid on things. I chilled out for a while.

River was also with me during this time and she told me this whole power thing was a bad idea.

I turned my attention to other things. Like going to the old movie theater and getting involved with a cast of people who did a certain cult movie thing. River did this thing with me, as well, and I also started to take her with me doing the time travel thing for a bit just to show her it was a fun thing to do. She never said she could do it, too. That she kept to herself but it did explain why we were so close. This would be also where things get weird again for me and a bit fucked up as well.

Things started going wrong. Lynn's daughter's boyfriend, they both lived with Lynn at this point, almost got killed by me a few times. Once with a chain saw that he got in the way of and the second time when he decided to get violent with everyone. That time I dropped him to the ground with a shovel and he was arrested when the cops got there. He was an ongoing problem for a long time.

Then my sister showed up unannounced. I had not even talked to her in over twenty years by this time. I shot her husband because he got out of his car, wanting to fight and they would not leave. There was more to this but I don't remember what it was. When the cops came, I left. River was there during this event and she went with me back to 1975 for a bit so I could figure out what to do with my life. Taking another life was nothing I ever wanted to do. I just assumed I killed him because he was silent and not moving when I left.

Did I mention that every time I did time travel that I rode my motorcycle? It seemed the best way to do things. I called it my TARDIS. I loved Dr. Who and chose the name The Doctor as my nickname whenever I went somewhere. Many times, when I would go into the past, my bike was all I needed to prove to everyone I was a traveler. Like during the civil war.

When we did go back to Lynn's house after a few days, Lynn's time, things got even worse. Lynn told me how I had just fucked her life up and that she did not want me around any longer. She didn't know how she was going to keep things together now that I was going to be gone, but she would figure it out. This was in 2018.

So, me and River decided to go places. We had gone places like 2036 and in that reality, the volcano at Yellowstone park went poof. Then on the other side of the globe in October, another super volcano did the same thing. It set the entire globe back 200 years. It was not the end of human civilization, but it did thin out the herd quite a bit. We left this time when things got too much to deal with and we both hated the cold from the small ice age that ensued.

2019 came and something called Covid-19, a coronavirus, was manufactured and released. In 2020 they claimed a global pandemic and the entire globe shut down and then again before year's end. All this for a virus that only kills ten people in every fifteen hundred. Yet no one had it in them to see what was really going on, that this supposed pandemic was about control and not a disease. However, things got out of hand and the mutated virus did things that ended up killing off almost everyone. The vaccine didn't do anything to help matters, either. I should note that what I had just told you about is the same reality where Yellowstone blew up. We were now in a different reality.

I left yet again. I went back to 1958. I had memories of living at the Commodore Perry Hotel. Built as a luxury hotel in 1927, this was one of the most extravagant buildings in downtown Toledo at the time, so I went back there. As I walked into the front revolving door and started to climb the stairs to the restaurant on the second floor, the door man spoke to me. He talked to me as if he already knew me. He told me everything was left as it was per my instructions and that I was living in the building next door, the Secor Hotel. This was a mind fuck at first because I was there for the first time as far as I was concerned. All I could think to do was just go with it and see what happened. This was going to be a strange ride.

Back to what I was talking about. The doorman had told me I should go check on my room, make sure everything was the way it should be and then come back over to where we were talking. So I did. When I got back to the Commodore, the door man took me up to the restaurant. This was cool and the first time in my timeline I had ever been to this place while this floor was open. In 2020, this floor had been closed since the '70's and no one seemed to know why. In truth, I think they all wanted to forget.

There was a bar and a dance floor. There was also a section where a piano sat and behind it were the instruments left there from a big band. The rest of the floor held tables to sit at and enjoy the music. There were also a few booths and couches. The whole place was carpeted and there were drapes on the big windows. Of course, there was also the hotel bar.

As I stood there taking everything in, I saw my friend River singing next to the piano. This gave me a what the fuck moment. I did not know

River could do the same thing I could. River noticed me right after the number she was singing and ran over to me, giving me a big hug. I asked her what she was doing there and she told me almost everyone was dead in 2022, that she could not find me so she came here. My thoughts immediately went to my and Lynn's granddaughter.

"2022? Do you know if things are okay with Lynn? What about Artemys?"

River got really quiet after I asked this. Then she told me to follow her. She took me to the side so she could talk to me with no one listening in. "I am so, so sorry Tigger. They are all dead. The CV vaccine killed them."

I fell to the floor and from that moment on, things were never right with me.

I asked in shock about the vaccine. She explained to me that after I left to come here, CV cases had exploded around Thanksgiving and in the rush to come up with a vaccine, mistakes were made. Furthermore, they forced everyone to get the vaccine or people would not be allowed to go back to work, or do anything else for that matter. So, people did just that. Most people believed in the governments of the world and never dreamed that harm would come from taking it.

River told me that 90 percent of everyone who took the vaccine ended up dying six months after doing so. The vaccine seemed to work at first but the side effects from it became too much and many died. If people already had an immunity to it, as some did, the vaccine they were forced to take would kill them almost immediately from anaphylactic shock. The governments, of course, kept this part quiet.

It took me the rest of the day to get over this and get right in my head. The next day, myself and River worked on a playlist of songs we were going to do together since this is how we were to pay our rent and eat. Things went smoothly for a few months and I was actually enjoying myself for a change.

From time to time, on our days off, we would go places in different times. Let me just say, vacations for us took on a whole new meaning. We went to Woodstock three times and watched the very first silent movie in what was real time for us. Once in a while, we would need to go back to 2019 or 2018 or whatever. I needed to get the right gasoline for my bike and get some money. So did River. We also had our cell phones still active so that we could get a hold of people for whatever reason. Everything worked out nicely until the last call I got.

In 2021, I had been gone for a while from Lynn's home. I got a phone call from her granddaughter, Artemys. I had the phone on just in case someone we knew would call me and I could get an idea just how bad things were getting in the world. The streets were becoming ghostly. Anyhow, Artemys told me how bad things were at her house while living with her mother and that she wanted to run away. I'm not going to go into it all since most of the conversation is about her begging me to come get her. I have to say that I had torn feelings about this. My heart went out to Artemys, and since I could never tell her no, I used the excuse that I needed to discuss all this with River. That way I could hang up.

So, I finished getting gas and everything else we were going to take back with us, be it for trade or so we could have food to eat that we could not get in 1958. The conversation turns to the phone call I just got and we talked about going to get Artemys at some length. I think the deciding factor was the fact that we already knew that within a year she would be dead so it would not influence anything big in the timeline. So it was agreed that we would go get her. I called her back and explained to her that we would come get her and the how and when.

I told Artemys that I wanted no one around in about 15 minutes and that she was to only bring a change of clothes and one stuffed animal.

She did follow my instructions, sort of. She only had the clothes on her back and she told me that was because she did not want to chance going back in the house and being stopped.

We took off like a bat outta hell and never went back to 2021. I think you can understand why. I then understood why in 2021 money in my account kept disappearing. I didn't know where it was going at the time.

Artemys was the sweetest little girl you could ever meet and very kind. She would always want to help out with things and she believed the best in everyone.

Back in 1958, Artemys was home schooled by River for obvious reasons. One being that we did not need Artemys telling people where she was from. That would have created problems for all of us we did not need. I also instructed Art to start calling me "Daddy" so that no one would question who she was, and we dyed her hair black. Though most people would think we were nuts if we talked about being from another time, some would take it to heart and the paranoia of the time was we knew that if the government found out there would be real trouble.

Paul Ieson

When we had to go somewhere without Artemys, there was someone we thought we could trust to leave her with. They had kids of their own and they knew and believed us about what had gone on since we told them a lot of it and proved it to them. I also had to apologize to them for being so vague about telling them things but, we had to protect people.

Things seemed to be going rather smoothly for a while and we were happy. Then one day while River and I were on stage doing our thing, who walked in but my mother at 16 with her parents and sister. From here on out, things got all fucked up though some of this would be my own fault. At that time I had no clue what was about to happen.

Chapter Three

During our music break, my mother walked up to me and River at the table we were sitting at and told us how awesome we were. River made the mistake of inviting her to sit down with us and tell us why she liked us so well. River, at this point, had no clue who this girl was and I had to just sit there silently and try to figure out just how I could get out of this crap.

My mother just went on from a kid's point of view to tell us about how much she liked us and how she wanted to be friends. River was eating all this up and said she would like to be friends, too. I sank back in my chair. River had no clue what she had just gotten us into. If I knew one thing about this, it was that my mother did not know how to leave anything alone and she would become a big pain in my ass.

I finally speak up and say that me and River need to talk about some stuff that was just between us. So my mother left the table. I told River what she just got us into and she started to freak a little bit. I managed to calm her down. This is no small feat when it comes to River. We then go back up on stage to finish out our set for the night. I wish things ended there but it was not my luck that evening.

Just as we were getting ready to leave and go home, my mother insisted that we sit with her family so she could introduce us to her parents. Man, was this a mistake. We should have made some excuse and just left, but we sat down at the table so we would not appear rude. Life would never be the same again.

Everyone introduced themselves and we made small talk for about fifteen minutes. This was when I had to begin to just do damage control and also try to find a way out of this.

My grandfather said, "Walk with me", and so I did. We left the building and went to the street. At least it was nice out and there was no one around to hear the conversation that was about to take place. Remember, I am only half human and my grandfather was full blown extra terrestrial. He knew exactly who I was.

His first question to me. "What are you doing here?"

There was no point in lying to this man, so I just came out and told him why we were here in this time.

"I honestly did not even consider what time I chose to live in. The furthest thing from my mind was meeting you all here. However, I do have to admit that it is good to see you and Grandmother again."

"Aright, so this is an honest mistake then. Fine. I will discuss this with your grandmother, and we will take things from there. I will let you know what is decided. Do not come to my house looking for an answer. I will find you."

We then walk back inside and say our good nights. River and I go home in silent mode. We did not speak to each other the rest of the night.

A few days later, we were up doing our music set. When I looked to the back of the restaurant and saw my granddad walk into the room, I personally was thinking that he would just tell me to stay away from his side of town and he would stay away from here. But this was not the case. Looking back, it would have been better that way.

He waited until we were done and came down to our normal table with our drinks already on them. We only acknowledged his presence as he walked up.

"Hi. After a very long discussion with my wife and some of our other people, we will have no trouble keeping our mouth shut about whatever upcoming events may hold. So, you two are welcome to become part of our lives. However, do not tell your mother or aunt anything at all. You will just be friends of the family and it will be easier to keep an eye on you as well."

I ordered my grandfather, Ed, a drink and said what was on my mind. "I don't know if that would be a good idea. We will talk about it and let you know. If you want to stick around for our next set, it's cool with me. I will play one of my original songs for you if you decide to stay."

River and I walked back onstage and started our next set. My grandfather said he enjoyed my song but that I should give up singing. I agreed.

River and I talked almost the entire afternoon after we were done working. We had our friend watch Artemys and we headed out. We got on my bike and headed over to my grandparents' house. No one really said anything about my bike, which is one of a kind at this time since I told everyone when they first saw it, that it was a custom build and left it at that. It was a lie but no one in '58 needed to know that.

When we got there, I pulled onto a side street and then told River that the house right across the main road from us was the place we had to go. This ended up being in our favor since my mother and her sister ran up to us. We told them we were looking for the house and they pointed out the way. I thought it made things look like we didn't know where we were going.

To my surprise, their house was not finished being built and the family is living in this huge garage. After all the polite welcoming and so forth, my grandfather said that since I was there, I could help with working on the house. It was a bit much for Ed to do all on his own. I did and we had a wonderful dinner that my grandmother made. Her name was Vera. I miss her cooking

This sort of thing went on for a few weeks. We would visit on the weekends and even took Artemys with us a few times. I thought it was a good idea to take Artemys because she was having a hard time adjusting and sometimes she would get home sick, bad. This worked out pretty well until Artemys let it slip to my mother that we were from a different time. This caused some issues for us all.

She still had no clue who I was but had threatened to go to her dad about what Artemys said. I didn't want to get into shit with my grandfather before I was even born, so I had to come up with something fast. I offered to take her some place in a different time just one time to shut her up. She accepted and this would become the biggest mistake of my entire life.

"The first place I took her was to 1929 so that she could witness the great depression. I thought this could be an educational thing for her at the time and it was. It was also a fuck up on my part. When we got back to her home, I learned that she was a liar even back then, not just from when I was growing up. She told me that if I did not take her places when she wanted, that she would tell her dad what I had done. All I knew was that I needed to talk to River to see how to get out of this one. I didn't want to go anywhere with my mother, I wanted to just stop joy riding through time because I knew at some point that nothing good would come of it.

Finally, I had enough of this woman trying to blackmail me and I told her this would be the last time we go anywhere. When we arrived, I gave her the order that she was not to leave my side and if she did, we would leave right then and there. This was my attempt at damage control. I took her to the day when Evel tried to jump the Snake River. However, what I told her did not work and she ran off. I spent over an hour looking for her. I found her inside a van. There was a guy trying to have his way with her and she was screaming my name over and over. As I creeped up on this dude, I saw another girl in the van who seemed to be tied up but was not moving. I also saw this fucker trying to get Cindy's clothes off. The only thing I saw to grab was a rock so I sneaked up behind this guy and smashed him in the head with it. He went down hard. Cindy gave me a big hug. She was pissed and crying and hurt all at the same time.

I turned my attention to the other girl. I untied her and instructed her to go find a cop, then turned my attention back to Cindy.

"Why the fuck did you bring me here?" I was trying to understand her through the sobbing. I said nothing at first.

"Why did you bring me here?"

"You asked to come here. Why are you yelling at me?" I had an idea, but was not sure. "This would not have happened if you had not run off."

"Just shut up and take me home."

"Okay. You going to be okay?"

"I can't talk to you right now. Just take me home."

"I told you to stay close to me. I told you not to run off, so what happened?"

"Just shut up and go."

When we got back to the house, Cindy was still not talking to me so I yelled for River and we went home.

When we got home, River said she noticed something was wrong with Cindy and asked me about it. I did not want to answer so I told her that I didn't want to talk about it and we just went on with our day.

The next day we went back over to see Ed and the rest of the family. I had to know how Cindy was doing after what happened. When we got there and pulled into the drive, Ed and Cindy walked out to greet us.

"Last night, Cindy came to me crying and telling me about the events of your last excursion."

"Ed, I told her to stay close to me. I don't even know what all happened."

Cindy was glaring evilly at me like she wanted me to die. Ed continued with what he had to say. "Cindy says she was almost raped while y'all were there and it is your fault. What say you?"

I suddenly am like, "What. The. Fuck!?" trying to find the words to say. "Ed. You know who I am. You also know what kind of person I am and that I would never do anything like that. I told her not to run off and to stay close. As soon as we got there, she ran off. Hell's Angels were there doing security for some fucking reason and then it all went bad. Many got hurt before we could get out of there. When I found her, she was in a van."

River stays silent.

Ed looks disappointed about the whole damn thing that has gone on. "I believe you, Tigger. I do. But I think I am going to have to ask that you go home and not come back here. For a while anyway."

Cindy speaks up. "You knew what was going to happen, you liar."

I lost it and said things I should never have said, but I was pissed. "Cindy, you are my mother, damn it! I would never, and could never, ever do something that would get you hurt. Sometimes you need to take responsibility for your own actions!"

I then started my bike, we said our good-byes, and we went home. River was still not saying a thing.

We arrived at home, went to our room and River picked this moment to lay into me and tell me how stupid I was over what just happened. I managed to calm her down but now she is not talking to me, either. I think it was her way of letting me know that I fucked up big time. This is the way she handles things a lot of the time. With the silent treatment.

Days go by without her saying a word to me outside of work. Artemys even asked me what was wrong but I could not respond to her about it. I just said I didn't know.

After this event blew over, things went rather smoothly for the next few months. River even hinted a few times about getting married and she moved in with me. I would blow this off because I thought she was joking. Then shit hit the fan and things got interesting again.

We were all in the restaurant of the hotel. River was off in the far corner, singing a song with the piano player. Artemys was off hanging out with her friends, just like any other morning. I saw five men walk in wearing black suits from my time, not the '50s and I knew they were trouble. I ran over to River and told her as calmly as I could that THEY found us and we had to go. Then I went to find Artemys and tell her the same.

We all walked over to get what stuff we were going to take with us and to figure out where to go. We were trying not to let anyone have a clue we were about to leave. Then Artemys said she did not want to leave and threatened to run off if we tried to make her. I went next door and asked my friend if Artemys could stay with them. I told them I would pay them whatever they wanted if they would take her in. They agreed and she stayed.

We gathered our crap and headed out to where the bike was parked. As I was starting my bike, the men in black saw us and ran towards us, yelling to stop. We ignored them and took off. Just before we jumped to another time, we heard gunshots.

We were in 1920, still in Toledo but at a place called Collingwood. It was just after the war and the plague. Collingwood, at this time, was owned by the Catholic church and, as we were to find out, it was being used to house homeless vets. We soon found out it was used for more than this. At first, we were in love with the place and offered the nuns our assistance in taking care of things around the place.

Paul leson

We had the intention of only staying about a week, helping out when we could to earn our keep and then we would go home. We could get back home within a few hours of leaving and everything would be just fine. Then again, things never went as planned. Since River and I were not married, we were given separate rooms to stay in and for the most part, we didn't see each other because of the work that we were assigned by the nuns. We did have our time off to be together, though.

About two days after we arrived, a friend of ours from our time walked in. Tarra was her name and River asked Tarra how she got there. Tarra said she had no clue how she got there or why she was even there until she was put in charge of the children. River asked about the children because we thought there weren't children at this place. Tarra said the children's home was over flowing and these were ones they had no room for since the epidemic and war. She added that things were not right with the kids because she is the only one they will come out of hiding for. They stayed hidden any other time.

A day later, Tarra convinced the children to meet with me and River. I was eager to see these kids and find out why they were so scared, thinking that I might be able to fix whatever was wrong. Again, I bit off more than I could chew.

Tarra took us up to the attic of the building, up above the auditorium where they had plays and held music concerts to raise money for the church. Anyway, in the attic there was a huge open part above all the rooms where the veterans were staying where the kids hid. There was no way to get up there but the kids seemed to have found a way they were not telling anyone about.

The children all came down from there and gathered around us. They explained to us what happened when the priest and the head nun caught a kid trying to sneak food. The Nun set things up as an adoption of the child but really the priest sold the kid into slavery most times, or the sex trade. He did not care. He just wanted the money. The kids also told us that sometimes, at certain times of the year, the priest would catch a kid and no one would ever see them again. They thought he was using them in some sort of ritual sacrifice.

Without saying a word, me and River looked at each other and in unison we told them that we were going to fix it and no one would hurt them anymore. How we were going to do this, we hadn't a clue at the moment, but we committed ourselves so we had to do something. Me and River agreed we would get together that night and talk about it. We told the kids they would see us soon and we went back downstairs to finish up our work.

A few days later, we met with the kids again. We told them about a children's home we could take them to in the middle of the night that was just over the border in Michigan and that they would be safe there. As safe as they could be in a children's home in that day and age.

As we were going down the main stairs to the kitchen, the head nun stopped us and informed us that we had until the end of the week and then they would not be needing our services any longer. We just got kicked out. But for what? We speculate that somehow, they knew what we were up to. So, I decided to step things up a bit without informing River. I found the priest who was up in his room and planned to call him out on his shit.

As I am standing outside of this priest's room, I hear the man on the other side say. "Come on in, Tigger. I have been expecting you." So, I enter and stand just on the other side of the door I close behind me.

He is sitting at his desk and he invites me to take a seat.

"I prefer to stand, thank you."

"As you wish," He says in a quiet and creepy voice. He continues, "I have to ask, sir. Just what do you think you are going to accomplish by coming up to see me? I know why you are here and it is not because Mother kicked you out."

"Forgive me for being blunt but I suppose I should get to the point," I lean over his desk. "I know what you are doing to the kids and I want you to stop."

"Oh? And just what do you think I am doing? Before you reply I should caution you with what you are about to accuse me of." He is still talking all creepy and also acting like he has the upper hand.

I back off a tad and lay into him. "I know you are selling the children to whomever wants them, be it into slavery or human trafficking, and hiding behind the church to do it. I also know about the rituals you are doing. That ends now, too."

He stands and walks around the desk towards me, admitting to it all. "Yes, Mr. Tigger, the great time traveler. Or should I say, Doctor? Oh, I know who you are. I know everything about you. I am selling off these worthless kids. As to the other things you think I am doing, that is my business and you will stay out of it, or else." He then sat back down.

Before I can say anything else, he said. "You have been warned. Please close the door behind you." I started to head out of the room and then stopped. I remembered a spell that was taught to me once by an old hoodoo woman and I cast it on him. This should have made him think he was having a heart attack but surprisingly, it did nothing.

"I do hate it when people don't listen to me. Don't say I didn't warn you." He snapped his fingers and I felt a big pop in the top of my head. I thought I could hear it happen as well. I got a bad headache and felt like I didn't know where I was or what I was doing. It lasted about thirty seconds.

"Now maybe you will take your leave of me and you might want to hurry. You would not want anything to happen to your Artemys."

That was unexpected. I had never met my match in magic. I was thinking I have to find River, but to my surprise she was on the other side of the door, listening in with the head nun. The guy threatened Artemys and part of me believed him. River said that by the look of things, she took it that it had not gone well. I just gave her a nasty look.

"I just got my ass kicked," I said.

"What? How?"

"I tried doing a spell on him and he countered it, doing something to my head. I am still having trouble focusing on what's going on. He also said something about Artemys."

"Oh, damn. How did he know anything about Artemys?" River asked, surprised.

"One of two ways, I think. Either he went in my head and found out about her or Tarra told him. What do you think?"

"That BITCH!" River said, horrified.

We got to my bike and rode off. As we did, we could hear one of the kids yelling out of the window, "What about us?" I had no choice but to ignore them.

Chapter Four

The one time I wished the aliens were around but they weren't, we kept going everywhere but back home. 1974, then 1936 and then 1927. On and on, we couldn't seem to get home. We knew that the priest did something to me. He messed with my ability to slip into whatever time I wanted to go to. This was getting on both of our nerves. So I asked River if she could help me in any way and it turned out that she was able to. We were now back in the beginning of 1960 and from what we can tell, we have been gone about 2 weeks. The thing that sucked was we ended up all the way across town, in what at that time, was the boonies.

As luck would have it, we got halfway to the hotel and the bike died. It didn't take too long to figure out that I was almost out of gas and t I had to turn the reserve on. We also decided that it was time to leave here and find a new place and time to stay. Things were just too slow and boring here.

We were here, but just like always, nothing went as planned.

So, we were running all over the damn hotel looking for Artemys, but everyone said they had not seen her in days. I went next door to talk to the guy that I left Art with to watch her until we got back. As luck would have it, he was home. He informed me that he threw her out a week ago because she did not do what she was told. I politely told him that Artemys had better be okay or his ass was mine.

I found River in the restaurant of the Commodore. She was standing next to a false wall where she heard fighting and a girl screaming to stop. I heard it and yelled at everyone else in the restaurant, "What? Are you all fucking deaf?? You people cannot tell me you cannot hear what is going on!" No one said a word. They just stood there with their heads up their asses.

I grabbed a chair and smashed it apart on the floor then used part of it to go through the wall. When we got inside this old room, River headed over to Artemys and I took off after the black kid that ran off as we entered the room. This kid had just hurt my little girl and if I got a hold of him, I was going to kill him.

River was kneeling over Artemys on the floor. "Sweetheart what happened? Why are you even here?"

"Daddy's friend, Mr. Williams, threw me out." Artemys was really weak and it was hard for her to speak.

"What?! Why would he do that shit for?" River was trying to hold back her anger for Artemys' sake.

"He said I was lying to him about doing what he told me to do when I wasn't lying. His daughter said she did it, when she didn't, and he believed her and kicked me out. He said he didn't care what happened to me." She was now having a real hard time breathing. "Where is Daddy?"

At this point I returned to both of them, but I did not think Artemys knew I was there.

"He is here, honey. He will be here in a minute." I tapped River on her shoulder to let her know I was there. "Look, honey, here he is." Art looked up at me and took her last breath. River and I embraced each other and began crying uncontrollably. I regretted taking off after that kid and knew this would haunt me for the rest of my days.

Some time passed before we came out of the hidden room and through the broken wall. When I got out into the main room carrying Artemys in my arms, I saw about 20 people standing there. All of them were silent, just looking stupid and I went off.

"Just what the fuck are you all staring at? Y'all gathered around here being nosy and you didn't even have the gumption to be bothered to see what was going on or to stop it. Did anyone bother to even call the cops? You know what?" I kept getting louder and louder, fighting with myself to keep the tears back. "I think you all need to just go the fuck home! As a matter of fact, I think this place is now closed permanently! And if any one tries to reopen this place, I don't care when it is, this place will burn to the ground. Try me and see what happens." I was so hurt and pissed.

Me and River walked over to my room next door. I placed Artemys on my bed and began stroking her long black hair. I had been doing this for quite some time, it was far after midnight. I finally got up off of the bed and instructed River to cut off my hair. She asked why and I told her I had been shamed. She grabbed a knife and did what I asked of her. When she was done, she asked me what to do with the hair. I told her I didn't care, so in the garbage it went.

River walked over to me. "So, what do we do now?"

"You don't have to come with me, but I think it is time that I go pay someone a visit." I had fire in my eyes and I knew it scared her so I tried not to show it.

"I think you should wait a little bit and cool down."

I said, "Fuck you" and ran out of the room to go next door.

By the time River caught up to me, I had already started to try and kick this guy's door down. River was telling me to chill out but I continued to make a scene. "You better open up, you son of a bitch, before I come in and kill your stupid ass!"

"Tigger! Stop before someone calls the cops." Now River was yelling.

Just as she stopped yelling, he opened his door. "What the fuck is your problem, Tigger?" I could see he was shaken.

I grabbed the collar of his nightshirt and pushed his ass back into his room, slamming him up against his wall. "You stupid mother fucker. You threw Artemys out and would not let her come back. Now she is dead. What the fuck do you have to say about that?" The guy just laid against the wall on the floor, stunned.

"You better start talking while you are still able." He was shaking so bad, I was thinking he was going to piss himself and then he did.

"Talk!" I screamed. About this time, I heard River running down the hall to try and stave off the cops and explain what happened.

Williams' voice was really shaky and I could hear the fear in the man. "I am so, so sorry Tigger. Never for a minute did I ever think she would be hurt. You have my deepest condolences and my apolog-..."

He never got to finish what he was saying because I decked him. "You better get your shit together and figure something out because I am not done with your ass yet." I went to River and told the cops they were needed in the room down the hall. We headed down and out of the building.

As we were on our way out, I instructed the doorman that under no circumstances whatsoever was anyone to go into my room until I returned. I headed out of the main door and we rode off on my bike. We drove in the direction of the Oliver House; it was a Civil War infirmary. President Lincoln stayed there for a few days. River asked where we were going and I told her we were going to see Lincoln and get him to change his mind about freeing the slaves. She said I was out of my mind and to stop. I ignored her and kept going. I was far from being in my right frame of mind at the moment.

Just before we slipped into 1859, River said she wanted to go home and I stopped the bike. I remembered we needed gas and spotted a gas station across the street so we pulled in there. "We will go home as soon as I am done doing what I intend to."

River's attitude flared up. "No. I mean home."

"What? You want to go back to 2023?"

"Yes. I don't think I can put up with you like this. I want to go home and pick up whatever is left to pick up after all the crap that went on. But take me to 2025. It should all be over by then."

"Okay, but we are going there first. I don't think it will take long. He already knows who I am."

She said, "Fine." Then she clammed up on me and I could get nothing else out of her.

When we pulled up to the building, we were greeted by some military personnel that were quite confused by the method of our transportation. It took me a while to explain what an iron horse was. I had to come up with an elaborate story about it and said that it was a classified government project. I was sort of proud that I could pull that story out of my ass.

The soldiers finally told us that Lincoln had left only the day before and told us the direction he was going. They said we could catch up with them somewhere down what would become Route 51. It seemed like a good thing that we could meet up with him and also have time to get something to eat since we had not eaten in a few days. River was silent most of the time.

When we left the Oliver House, travel was a bit slow. Ever try to ride a motorcycle down a wet dirt road? It took almost 45 minutes just to make it through what little there was to the east of Toledo. We kept riding down future Route 51 but could only go about 10 miles an hour at best. I hoped we could meet up with someone or find a place to stay the night before it got dark. River was still silent.

So, the road dried out allowing me to go faster. I rode up on the only house on 51 for miles and we decided to stop.

"I know this house!" River said nothing. "Ain't this the house that is right across the street from the dollar store? I think it is."

River spoke up. "Looks like it to me. That would mean we are in Millbury. I wonder what Lynn's property looks like in this time."

"You just had to remind me, didn't you?" I got somber again.

We rode up to the house and everyone came out to greet us. The children there were very interested in the bike and kept asking for a ride while me and the man of the house talked. He made them get back in the house and I asked him about staying the night. He agreed to let us stay in the barn. He said we should not have any problems with the animals and then gave me an oil lamp to use.

As we entered the barn, the guy showed us where we could bed down on some hay against the wall. I find out the guy's name is Sam. The same name of the guy who owns this place in our time. An interesting note to keep but I was really too exhausted to have much conversation in me and wanted to sleep.

Sam blurts out. "Where y'all from?" I waited a minute to reply.

"Up the road a bit, by the river." River spoke for the first time since we arrived.

"East Side." I said not thinking.

"Where?"

"FrogTown. Over by the Oliver House." River tried to fix my stupid.

"I have never seen anything quite like that thing you came up on. What did ya call it? Iron horse?"

River spoke again, to my surprise. "Yup, that there is one of them government secrets no one is supposed to know about." It's funny when River is trying to talk hillbilly.

Sam started to get irritated. "Now just hold on here a minute. I may not be the smartest person in town but I know one thing, you people don't belong here. You dress funny, in clothes I have never seen before and your mannerisms are all wrong for people from around here."

"My apologies, sir. We do not wish to come across as rude. You have been good to us and we are grateful. I can be straight with you if you so choose but I have to warn you that you may not believe us."

We all sat down on a few old logs in the barn. I lit a cigar with a lighter and then tossed it to Sam.

"You are correct. We are not from here. We are from another time. Take a look at what I just gave you. That's now yours. It's called a lighter, an easy way to start a fire any time you might need to. My Iron horse is called a motorcycle and it's transportation from my time. We are from 2023 and we came back here to talk about some things with the President. I would really appreciate it if you would keep what I just told you between us."

Sam got up and walked to the door. "I am going to have to talk to my wife about this. You can stay here tonight. I can keep my mouth shut, if you like. Not like anyone would believe me anyway." He walked to his house and went inside. We heard him yell as he went in the door, "Martha! You're not going to believe this..."

"Glad that's over with. All I want to do is sleep." River laid down on a blanket I had in the bike's saddle bag. I laid my head down, wishing I had a real bed to sleep on.

Three a.m. came much too early. Sam's damn rooster woke both of us up in a way that, had I had the money to replace the bird, I would have ripped its face off and gone back to sleep. I had forgotten that this was a farm and farms had chickens. If there are chickens, there are roosters. So, this was not a good morning for me.

I lit the oil lamp and took it upon myself to break the silence between us. "Do you want to go back with me when we are done here, take care of Artemys and get your stuff? Or, do you just want to go to 2025?"

River was quiet for a few minutes. She was having a hard time waking up, too. "Do you really want to talk about this now, dear?"

"Yes. Why not?"

"Fine. I think we should leave here now and go back and not worry about doing whatever it is you want to do." River, I could tell, was trying to be nice about what was on her mind.

"But..."

River cops an attitude. "I'm talkin'. Shut up and let me finish. I get how you were all fucked up in the head yesterday. I was, too, but I really think it is time to leave here. Yes, I wanna be there to take care of Artemys. Why would you even think you would have to ask me that?"

I sat there in the hay and thought about my reply. If I said this wrong, River would flip out on me. "I'll tell ya what, I will take what you say under consideration. I know you have a point with what you are saying, but I really want to do this."

"I guess that is all I can ask for at the moment." She sat back against the wall and pouted.

About this time, the farmer noticed that our light was on and walked out to the barn and through the door.

"Good morning."

"Hello," we said in unison.

"I, well me and the wife, thought you two could use a good breakfast and thought we would invite you to eat with us."

I said, "Sure".

River replied, "Yes, we would like that very much, Sam, thank you." We three all went to the house.

As we walked in, the smell of food permeated the first floor and I hoped I could get through this without being rude.

Sam stood back up from the head of the table. "We are honored to have these guests with us at meal time and we give thanks for this food and conversation. I, we, also have some questions for you two, if you don't mind." He sat again.

I wondered what I was going to pull out of my ass this time. "Ask anything you want but please understand I may not be able to answer all of your questions."

"I understand, Tigger." The farmer said, smiling.

We all dug in and started eating. Damn, it was good cooking. I didn't think I had eaten like this in the morning in years. "Ma'am, this is very good. Thank you so much."

Sam's wife replies, "You are very welcome. I am glad you enjoy it, but it is nothing really."

Sam speaks up. "Please tell us again where you are from. I had a difficult time explaining it to my wife and my kids want to hear about it, too. After all, they watched you ride up to the house."

"Sure. I can do that. We are from the year 2023. We were living in 1960 but something very tragic happened and we are now here. We came to talk with the president about a matter I cannot discuss at this time."

"We can tell you are not from here. I guess the real question I have is how did you get here?"

I took another bite of my food so I could stall a minute while I thought of something. "I take it that if I say it is classified, that won't be good enough for you." I said with a smile.

"No, sir."

"Okay, then. There is a device on my iron horse called a flux capacitor that allows us to go where we want to. I don't know how it works; I just know that it does."

The farmer and his wife looked at each other for a second and the farmer continued, "You are not the first travelers we have had like you two. The thing is, you all give the same answer. Do you people from the future all do this for a past time or what?" No one was eating now and everyone was hanging on my words. I got the feeling that things were not what they appeared to be.

"Not to my knowledge, it is not. As far as me and River know, we are the only ones that do this. Let me ask a question, sir. Just how many other people from different times have you met?"

Sam and his wife looked at each other again and gave each other a nod yes. "Well, us for one and a handful of others." This took us off guard and they could tell.

"No fucking way." I muttered to myself not realizing I spoke aloud until River yelled, "Tigger!"

"Sorry for swearing."

"It's okay. You should hear me when I am alone." Sam was smiling and holding back a laugh. "I will also add here, Tigger, that you do not need to steal movie quotes when you talk with us." Me and River's mouths were hanging open.

Silence hung over the table for a little bit and we all finished our food. Sam invited us into the living room, so we followed.

Paul leson

"What is it that you guys did in 1960?" Sam's wife asked. Her name was Berta, by the way.

"We were musicians at the commodore. It was a living." I said.

Sam asked, "Why were you in 1960?"

I reply with a statement that can narrow down where Sam and his wife came from. "Covid 19."

"Ah, the same reason we are here. Who would have known a vaccine would be so deadly?" Sam lit his pipe. "If you have not noticed, we have a piano over there. Do either of you play?"

I said yes, a little bit, and sat down. River walked over and I started to play the only Eagles song I know, Wasted Time. I thought they would get into this one and River sang.

Chapter Five

The few days we stayed with Sam and Berta were relaxing and a nice change of pace. Sam convinced me to stay and any argument that I had he put to rest saying I had a bike and could catch up to them any day I wanted. I knew he was really hoping I would pull my head out of my ass. He finally got me to tell him what I was planning and he did not like my plan too much. He said that he did not think it was a good idea trying to change the time stream but didn't know how to stop me.

I finally asked Sam how they got to this time. He tells me that he was driving down Woodville road back home and the next thing he knew he was in this time. He said he didn't know how he did and, from the way he explained things, I couldn't think of how, either. He said this was his home in 2020 but he had to build this place to have somewhere to live in this timeline. It made me think about the humor of the universe.

River and I gave hugs and said our good-byes, then took off east on 51. It was not long after we left Sam's that we rode through what appeared to be a blinding bright flash of light and then everything was different. The road became a log road, not dirt and there was swamp all around us. The natives here called this place the Black Swamp.

We could see from about a quarter mile away that there appeared to be people, how many we couldn't tell. We both said "What the hell" and we rode up to them to ask them some questions. This startled the men, who were all Confederate soldiers, and they took a defensive stance towards us. I rode us up as slow as I could without falling, and when we got really close, I shut off the bike and got off. The men were all still kneeling and pointing their rifles at us.

The soldier on the one horse they had ordered me to stay where I was.

I raised my arms up above my head. "I assure you, sir, we mean you no harm and we have no weapons." Then I lowered my arms but not all the way.

The lieutenant on the horse asked first off, "What is that... thing... that I see you on?"

This was the time to pull out everything that I could and make things as believable as I could so I could get us out of this situation. I did not have a good feeling about it. "This is my iron horse. It is something that is top secret and owned by the U.S. government. Myself and the lady here are scientists and are on the project to develop this thing." Well, what was I supposed to say? That we were time travelers? That would have probably got us shot.

River got off the bike and walked up beside me. She took my arm but stayed silent. I whispered an assurance to her that I would do my best to get us out of this. She just gave me a look like she didn't believe me. I didn't believe me, either. I was not sure just how to deal with this. I only knew that I had no choice and was going to take it minute by minute since things seemed unpredictable at the moment.

"I just have one question, sir, and we will be on our way. We seem to be lost. Where are we?" I immediately regretted asking this.

The lieutenant spoke up with a puzzled look on his face. "You are on the main road heading into FrogTown, about 30 miles out. If I may ask, just what are you doing out here anyway?"

"What year is this?" I ask.

"1863. What an odd question, sir." Damn. We time slipped and didn't even know it. What the fuck?

"About your last question to me, sir. It's classified. I am sorry. I don't wish to sound rude but I am not allowed to tell anyone without clearance." We walked over to the bike and got on. Before I started it back up, I yelled, "As far as I am concerned, this never took place." I started the bike and attempted to pass by the group of men. River raised her hand and waved saying, "See ya, boys."

Just as we passed the men, a shot rang out. It startled the hell out of us. I see one of these fuckers just shot my gas tank. I immediately stopped and got off the bike screaming my ass off. I did not handle this well. "Just what the hell is your problem? We are no threat to you. I can't believe you shot my horse!"

The lieutenant speaks up, "What do I call you, sir?"

"Doctor. I am the Doctor."

"Doctor. I ordered my man to shoot. I am not so sure I should let you leave."

"What! Why? We are not a threat to you and I said I would not even say anything about running into you." I shut off my bike and looked at the damage.

The lieutenant climbed off of his horse and walked over to me.

"Do you realize that you may have just stranded us here?" I knew he knew I was angry.

He spoke up, "Sir, I do not know any form of our government that would be responsible for this thing here." He was pointing at the bike. "Furthermore, I do take you for a threat because I cannot tell how this would even work in the fashion that it does and it looks like something out of the future." Maybe this guy wasn't as stupid as he looked.

River chimes in. "The future! That is just preposterous." I look at her.

"Ya. What she said."

The lieutenant turned to walk away and gave his men the order to relax. "I propose that we all take a few minutes and talk about our

85

situation over there in the clearing." His men all walked over to where the lieutenant ordered them and we reluctantly joined him.

We all found somewhere to sit, be it a rock, a log or the ground. The lieutenant remained standing and began to ask me questions about us, demanding answers. Basically, he decided that he would turn himself and his men around and go back to where his regiment was supposed to be. He said he would let his commanding officer decide what to do about us. We were prisoners.

This did not make me happy and River, I could tell, was now very upset. So, I excused myself by saying that I was going to get water from my saddle bag, and I did. I had lied about being unarmed. Well, sort of lied. Neither River nor myself were carrying a gun. But when I reached into my bag, I also grabbed my revolver. I hid the gun in the waist of my pants after loading it and then walked back to River with water bottles showing in my hand.

While I handed River the water, I told her what I was planning. I was going to shoot our way out. These losers only had rifles that fired one shot at a time. I could take them out in 30 seconds. So, we took nice long drinks of our water. Then River ducked behind a fallen tree and I pulled out my gun. At this point. I wasn't worried because I am a fairly decent shot.

I started shooting, always moving so I wouldn't get shot. I ended up hitting all nine people and thought that I killed them all. I was wrong. When I walked over to where I last saw River, I found out what everyone says was true. You didn't hear the shot that got ya but you did feel it. River screamed and I went down on my knees. I had been gut shot.

To our surprise, Union soldiers ran up to see what was going on. As it turns out, the Union knew about the Confederates traveling up toward the river and they were sent to stop them. This was the good news. Some of the men knew me and called me by name but I did not remember them. I asked for someone to make sure River was okay and I found a log to lay myself on. I was gut shot and this was not a good thing.

Everyone stayed with me for a few hours and even tried to get me to let them carry me back to the Oliver house. River was with me and she tried to talk me into it, as well. I turned down the offer to be taken back with them. It was false hope. In that time, there was no fixing me. I was done.

River did not want to accept this and pleaded with me. I instructed one of the men that they were to take River with them and make sure she got anything she needed. I said my goodbyes to the men and to River. She wanted to stay but I wouldn't let her. She tried anyway. No one would leave. It was sort of nice that people were concerned and I would not have to die alone.

I had been suffering through this shit for nine hours. Someone gave me some whiskey but it didn't help much and I just wanted it over with. I was finally going to die and it didn't look like I would be rescued by the aliens this time. That's what I get for thinking...

When everyone was asleep and the fire was almost gone, there was this bright ass flash of white light and I was on an alien ship. Questions were running rampant in my head and I was not happy. The aliens fixed me, damn it! The first thing I was able to get out of my mouth to the gray ass drone bitches was "Where is River?" Then they allowed her to walk in the room.

Chapter Six

The room we were in was dimly lit and a metallic gray color. The room was empty other than the table I was on. It was quite warm, so much so that it seemed to zap our energy. It was also surprisingly quiet. There were four gray aliens in the room with me and River. They stood about four feet tall.

River said under her breath. "Are we where I think we are?"

"Yes. I have been here a few times before but this is the only room on the ship I ever remember being in."

One of the aliens began to speak but I could not tell which one it was. These guys spoke with their minds and not their mouths. I could only assume who I was speaking with because one genderless asshole walked towards me. "It is nice to be able to see you again, Tigger. We apologize for not getting you out of your unfortunate situation sooner. It took us a while to find you because you were slipping uncontrollably into timelines." I was surprised to discover River was able to hear this conversation.

"What was that snap I heard and felt in my head? Was it that priest's magic?" Those were my first questions. "Are we done now? Can I go home?"

"No, my friend. You had a small stroke. That is why you were having so much trouble focusing on anything. We have repaired your condition and you should be fine." These emotionless creatures made it so hard to read anything between the lines, it seemed pointless to try, but I tried anyway.

River spoke up. "So, what now?"

"We have decided to place you back in 2005. Since you already know the outcome of things, this will give you an advantage and allow you to change things."

River spoke again. "Why are you doing this for us? What is in it for you?"

The honesty of these grays was unbelievable. They would tell you anything and not lie at all. "What is in it for us, River, is that we get to study the effects of any changes that will occur from reliving things. We wish to find out if you will change the timeline at all inside the point in which you are placed and the people you know."

"So, Tigger is right. You are treating us like lab rats. I don't think I wanna play." River was getting pissed and I didn't blame her.

"I am afraid you do not have any choice in the matter. This conversation is over." The alien nodded his head at the other short fuckers. There was a bright flash of light and River and myself appeared on the bank of the Maumee river. It was summer in the year 2005.

End reality one

River picked up a rock and skipped it across the water. "So, here we go again," comes out of her mouth. I remain silent. For about 10 minutes we said nothing to each other. We just stared across the river at the downtown area. Finally, River spoke up. "I don't know about you but I'm not going through this shit again."

"Me, neither. I don't care what them alien fucks try to do or have to say." I stood and searched for a cigar. "Hey, let's go get some food and figure out some shit."

River turned to me and said, "Fine." We walked over the blue bridge to the Oliver House for some good food.

We were both starving so we said nothing to each other at first. Then River broke the silence. "So?"

"So, what?" I said with my mouth half full.

"So, what are we going to do? Are we just going to go through all of this crap again? 'Cause I, for one, am not happy with doing that."

I put my food down. "Ya know when I was really happy, River?" She gave me a blank stare. "The only time I was ever really happy was at the Commodore. Why don't we just go back there? We know what we did wrong and we just won't do that stupid shit again."

River looked up at me and with a full mouth said, "I'm in, what the fuck? It's not like there is anything here for us. Oh, ya. Before I forget. I keep meaning to ask you why do you go by Tigger anyway, Mr. Paul."

"What? You haven't figured that one out yet? Tiggers bounce and with all the shit I have been through, and keep bouncing back from, they call me Tigger."

All she said was, "Okay", and started eating again. We finished lunch and then talked about how we were going to get back to 1959.

Here is a mind fuck for you, and for us as well. When we stepped out of the restaurant, there was my bike in the parking lot. I knew it was my bike because back in the other timeline, I was nowhere near Toledo in the summer of 2005.

"How the hell did this get here? River asked, holding back a laugh.

"I haven't a clue and don't care." In truth, I was a bit puzzled, too.

"Why do I feel like I am being led by the nose?"

"I don't know but I sort of get that feeling, too." Then River jumped on the back of the bike.

The first thing we did was ride over to the military surplus store. We picked up sleeping bags, a water distiller and other stuff we think we may need if we get stuck back in civil war times again. My bike seemed to be fixed but there was no gas in it so we went to get it. I also picked up gas treatment so I wouldn't have to come back to this time to get it. At least that's what I was thinking anyway. The weird thing was, when we opened the bags on the bike to start putting all the crap in them, the one thing in them was my hand gun. This didn't look right to us. Why would the aliens fix the bike and only leave the gun in it unless they wanted me to use it or see if I would? River wouldn't touch the thing. She hated guns.

We went back to 1960. I know I said we were going to 59 but we changed our minds. We wanted to end up back at the Commodore just after we left to go to Collingwood so that we can change the outcome with Artemys and keep her from dying. But we wanted to get there after the men in black left. As it stood, I still could barely function over her death.

"What are we going to do when we show up?" River had a pertinent question that I had forgotten to think about.

"Off the top of my head? We should be there to stop us from coming in the building, to tell them, us, what happened and send them off in another direction. It's an idea. What do you think?" We had not even walked through the door of the hotel yet, we were still standing by my bike. Our conversation was cut short because Artemys ran up to greet us.

"Daddy! River!" She gave us both a big hug.

I scooped Artemys up off the ground, yelling, "Baby girl!" and started crying.

"Daddy, what's wrong? Why are you crying?"

"Nothing, Sweet Pea. Nothing at all. I am just so happy to see you, is all." I put her back down.

We walked up to the restaurant where the door man greeted us. He smiled and said nothing as we passed him. We found a place to sit and continued talking for a while.

Artemys and River walked over to our rooms next door, but I remained seated. I was thinking about how I was going to treat Williams. You remember. The guy that I left Artemys with and he kicked her out of his house. After what happened, I had an extreme dislike for him. But since that incident had not happened, and wouldn't if I had anything to do about it, I could not take anything out on this guy since he had not done anything. I could only watch him and know better when it comes to allowing him to watch Artemys anymore. That goes double for the kid that lied on Artemys.

I had just been sitting, having a few drinks and fighting myself over shit. I was both depressed and happy at the same time and I didn't know what to do about it. I knew what was coming in two weeks and was hoping we could change the outcome. Then River and Artemys walked up on me.

River sat on my lap, something she didn't normally do. "Why are you still sitting here?"

"I don't know. Just haven't felt like moving, I guess."

"I'm hungry," Artemys said. "Can we get something to eat?"

"Yes, Hun. I am, too." River waved an employee over and asked if it would be too much trouble to find someone to take our order and that we would eat in the restaurant.

"For you guys? Yes, ma'am. I will do that for you." She took our order and we had a great dinner.

After we were done with the food, I asked Artemys about the room that the kids go into. I told her I thought they used it as a fort or something. She denied it at first, until I pointed to the wall across the room from us and told her that it was right there. She admitted that there was a room but she didn't know it was right there. I made her promise to never go back there ever again. She reluctantly agreed and asked why. I told her, "Just because I said so." We spent the rest of the night listening to the act on stage.

Chapter Seven

I t had been about two weeks and things were going rather smoothly. That is, until the day me and River had been worried about. We finished our music set early and River headed over to what was now our room because we were living together. She wanted to make sure Artemys was there. We had made it clear that she was not to leave the room on this night for any reason.

I follow her outside so I can catch us returning from that oh-so-fun last reality. When they pull up to the hotel, they are both looking at me like "What the fuck?" I could see this was going to be interesting. I played it out at the start like that Dr. Who episode. We both did.

I walked over to them as they stopped their bike and my other self got off the bike.

"What?"

I yelled, "What?"

"Wait. Doctor? What!"

"No Way. What?"

"That means... Wait. What?"

The other River almost fell off the bike, she was laughing so hard. She pulled it together enough to slap the other me upside the head.

"Get a grip." This was me, if you lost track in all that craziness. "I don't have time to explain. I pulled this out of my ass. I need to go through our childhood timeline and tell Cindy that it never happened and why. Or tell her that he, us, as a kid is not you or whatever the fuck. We have to clear this all up."

He got back on his bike and said, "Will do."

Just then River ran across the street and took me by the arm. "We have to go. Now!"

I looked back at them as I was being pulled and said, "Okay. Bye."

We passed the doorman on the way inside. He said, "What the hell." I yelled back at him, "Me and River both have twins." He said nothing after that and just looked puzzled.

"Artemys is not in our room." River was frantic.

"Damn it."

We ran up to the wall just like before, listening to see if we could hear anything going on. We heard screaming and yelling from two people. We also hear fighting.

"Time to break the wall again. Let's just hope." River grabbed a chair and smashed it into the wall, breaking through it. "We're coming, Artemys, just hang on."

Artemys was laid out on her back on the floor grabbing her arm and crying. We asked her what happened, knowing what had taken place. "Betty came over and talked me into coming here to play. She said she already talked to you and that you said it was okay, Daddy. She was here for a little bit and she left. She said she would be right back. Then this boy came in and tried to have sex with me. I beat his ass like you taught me to. My arm really hurts."

"River, check on that fuck stain over there." She did, but didn't say a thing. I could tell by the look on her face he was dead.

"Is he okay, River?" Artemys was genuinely concerned.

I told her not to worry about it, we would take care of this, and all three of us walked out of the hole in the wall this time.

River and I were so happy that things worked out this time. We never considered that it changed the entire timeline but then I don't think we cared, either.

There were about 20 people out here in the restaurant, all gathered around acting concerned. The doorman said he called the police. I thanked him then gave River a look. River and Artemys are still crying over this event. It was very loud in the restaurant and I told the doorman that we would be outside getting some air. He nodded, giving me confirmation that he heard me, and we walked out.

"Let's get the hell out of here for a while. I don't want to deal with the cops just yet," River told me as I lit a cigar.

"Yeah, me neither. This can only end up being a mess."

River gave me a kiss on the cheek, grabbed Artemys' hand and headed over to the bike.

"Sounds good to me," I agreed and we rode away from downtown. We intended to go to the park down by the river in the south end near the zoo. We wanted time to relax and think about what we wanted to do next. This was all great and we were having a good time riding until there was a flash of light and we were back on the road where I was shot. This time my bike stalled out and would not restart.

"Them damned aliens," I yelled. We pulled off to the side of the road and could see the Confederate soldiers about a quarter mile up the road. I looked around to see if there was a place we could hide but there was none. There was only a clearing next to us off the road so River and I pushed the bike over there.

"Daddy, where are we?"

I didn't answer her. "River, this time let's do something a bit different. How long did it take the Union soldiers to get here last time?"

"About three hours. Why? What are you thinking?"

"Get off the bike. I am going to hide it over here in these trees and we can just hang out over here, hidden, and hope they walk past us." I opened my saddle bag, took my gun out and put it in my waistband.

"And if they don't?" River was not enthused over this idea.

"Can we stall them until the Union gets here?"

About 10 minutes later, one of the Confederates walked into the clearing. "Yes, Lieutenant, they are here." They all walked to where we waited.

"Well, well, well. What do we have here? You folks are a long way from anywhere, ain't ya? Sit down boys, I think I am going to have a talk with our new friends here."

"What kind of uniform are these men wearing, Daddy?" Artemys just had to say something.

"These are soldiers, honey, and those are Confederate uniforms. You know who the Confederates are, honey. You read about them in school." I was a bit condescending when I said this to her. Artemys knew better than to speak again, so she stayed silent the rest of the time.

River spoke and I could hear a devious tone in her voice as she said, "How can we help you, boys? You seem to be far away from home, yourselves."

One of the men found my bike. "Sir. I found it. It's over here. I have never seen anything like it."

"Let me see." The lieutenant walked over and took a long look at it. He then looked back at me. "Just what, in all that is holy, is this?"

"That sir, is my TARDIS." I got a big shit eating grin, wondering if a TV show will get us out of this.

"Your what? What, pray tell, is that?"

I walked over to the man. "My TARDIS."

"What is that?"

"Oh, please forgive me. I suppose I do need to explain." I reached past him into one of the bags and pulled out some water. "Water, sir?" He says no. "TARDIS. Time And Relative Dimensions In Space, is what it stands for." The guy was looking at me with great interest. "You, sir, are looking at a genuine time machine."

"No, you must be joking."

I had just found my stall tactic; this should be fun. "We are time travelers who are lost."

"Please forgive my language, ma'am. That has to be the most asinine thing I have ever heard in my entire life." The lieutenant was giving me a stern look.

"Now hang on, sir, and let me try to explain everything before you dismiss what I say." I glanced at River. She was hanging on every word I said. I think she thought this was funny or something.

I opened the bags of the bike and started pulling stuff out to show the man. Like a flashlight and a lighter to start. "Have you ever seen anything like this?" I handed them to him.

"I should say not."

"How about this?" I pulled out my cell phone and powered it up. Then I turned on a movie I had saved on the phone.

"What is this called?" he asks.

"That, sir, is what is called a video."

"Very interesting." The guy took a seat next to the bike. His men were wondering what had gotten into their lieutenant. He called his sergeant over to watch the video.

"Holy Mother Mary," was all that came out of the sergeant's mouth.

I kept these guys distracted for a few hours. Then I started to run out of things to say. So River came up with the idea of telling stories and that seemed to work for a while. By this time, we were all sitting around in a circle, with a fire going in the center. It was probably afternoon, but I couldn't trust the clock on my phone.

Finally, the lieutenant took to his feet. "Well, all this is very interesting and I must say, Doctor, that you tell a good story or two. However, this is what is going to happen. We are going to take your TARDIS, in the name of the Confederacy, of course, and we are going to shoot you. Here where you sit." Things suddenly got very intense.

"I don't think you are going to shoot anyone." The voice came from the road. No one had noticed the Union soldiers walking up on us. I took a deep breath of relief.

The Confederates turned around to see who spoke then they all put their hands up. The lieutenant of the Union army walked up. "It would seem as though you got yourself in a bit of a pickle, Doctor." He declared that the Confederate soldiers were under arrest in the name of the Union. "Is there anything we can do for you, my friend?"

"Lieutenant Stanford Smith, my old friend. How the hell are you, sir?" I stand up to greet him.

"I am well, Doctor. It is a surprise to see you here. And who are these two fine ladies with you?"

I motion them both to get up. "This is my daughter, Artemys." She is standing in front of me. "This is River Song."

River greeted him so Stanford continued. "I have heard so much about you, Miss River. It is good to finally meet you."

She smiles, "All good, I should hope."

107

"Yes, Ma'am..." My friend was cut short in his conversation by the sound of a gunshot. Artemys screams and so does River. River thinks Artemys has been shot and so does Stanford because there is blood all over her back. This is not like last time. "No. Nope guys, it's me that got hit." I leaned over and hit the ground.

River screamed, "No! Not again!" She dropped to her knees beside me and so did Artemys.

"Daddy, are you okay?"

I never felt pain like this in my life. The musket ball bounced off my bottom rib and ripped through my guts, hitting my pelvic bone. "Holy shit, does this hurt. Anyone got some whiskey?"

A soldier said he did and River got up long enough to retrieve it from him. "It's okay, Tigger. It's going to be okay. We will get through this." River did not realize this time how bad it was. Artemys couldn't say much because she was crying her eyes out. About this time, one of the soldiers walked the guy that shot me over.

"This is the man that did it, Doctor." Stanford cut him off. "Do you want me to shoot him for you, Doctor?"

I was chugging whiskey like I never had to kill the pain but it wasn't helping any. "No. Let me." I reach around my waist and pull out my gun.

"Mister, I didn't mean to shoot you. I was aiming for the lieutenant."

"Like it fucking matters. I should just drop you now."

Artemys was crying uncontrollably but managed to speak. "No, Daddy. He said he didn't mean to." I handed the gun to River and told Stanford to do what he wanted to with him, just not in front of Artemys.

I was bleeding out bad and it finally occurred to River that I was not going to get out of this one. "Just hang in there, sweetie. Them damn aliens may just help us out again."

I started coughing up blood. "I don't think they are coming."

"Daddy, I don't want you to die. He's not going to die, is he River?"

All River could say was, "I don't know honey."

We did not notice that Stanford and a few of the other men walked the idiot out to the road and away from us but we did hear the gunshot.

"Did they just kill that man, River?"

"Yes, Artemys." Then Art cried even harder.

I feel my time coming fast. "Artemys?"

"Yes, Daddy?"

"I need you to do something for me. I need you to take care of River for me."

"Okay, Daddy."

"Artemys, I love you so damn much. I love River, too, but you mean more to me than life itself."

"I love you, too, Daddy. Daddy! Daddy!" Artemys was now frantic, crying and shaking me. "No, Daddy! No, please don't go." I was gone.

River insisted that Stanford and his men give me a burial. Everyone spent the night in the spot we were in and the next morning they did what River asked. River had a few men help her get my bike back on to the road and she said her thank yous and goodbyes. Then Art and

River rode off. Stanford and his men watched them ride into the distance and disappear.

Artemys and River made it back to 1950. River ended up with this rich guy who was in the oil business and lived in New York City, though she did not marry him. He had no one to leave his money to and since River did not care a thing about money, he left it all to her. She did rather well in the oil business. When she died at 51 in 1966, Artemys inherited a rather large sum of money from her. She did get married but her husband could not have children so they adopted a few kids. Artemys returned to the Commodore in 1969 when the Commodore Perry Hotel closed its doors and became the Commodore Perry Apartments. She went back to relive the good times with me and River, I suppose. She died in her sleep at 103 and was buried in Forest cemetery. But the story does not end there. I will tell you more at the end of this story.

End reality Two

find myself in a room that is all white. It is a round room or, I should say, the wall surrounding the outside of the room is a circle with no exit or windows. There is a white desk in the center of the room and a few chairs around, here and there. I have been here before. The last time I went through all the crap I did and got into shit. I don't want to be here but this is not my choice. This is the afterlife.

A woman appears before me on the other side of the desk. Then Arron, my mother, appears and we all sit down. Beverly, the woman sitting across from me, speaks. "Well, I think we all know why we are here."

"I told you, Bev, I was not lying. I told you what he did."

"That will be enough out of you, Arron. I will deal with you when I am done with the Doctor. I don't want to hear another word from you now. Should I call you Tigger? I know, I will just call you Paul, since that is your name." Beverly has a real stern tone in her voice as if she does not wish to be dealing with us.

"Hello, Bev. What did I do this time? I did the best with the cards I was dealt."

"Oh, let's see." Suddenly a few papers appear that she picks off the desk, all with my name on them. "Well, it says here that you almost killed one reality. You created a few more realities. You played music in other timelines and that should not have been done. You gave advice to certain people that originally were not supposed to come up with things and that disturbed the timeline, too. Then there is the matter of Artemys. Do I really need to go on?"

I sit back, light a cigar I pull out of thin air and speak in such a way that Bev knows I do not wish to be here. "In my defense, ma'am, them damn aliens had a lot to do with everything. Myself and River were thrown into places we did not belong a lot of the time."

"Leave it to you to try and use that. Ya, we know about the grays. We just don't know how to deal with them yet. But do go on. This should be interesting." Bev is now leaning on the desk with her chin in her hand listening intently.

I move towards her, as well. "Artemys died from CV so we didn't think there would be any harm done to the timeline if we went and got her."

"You got her too soon, had you waited until just before she was sick then everything would be good, but you didn't. That created a new timeline. Would you please get rid of that damn cigar?" Beverly "requesting" me to get rid of the cigar is more of an order than an option so I do just that. "Go on."

"How can you make me responsible for changing the timeline when we were plopped in 1863 more than once against our will? We did our best not to affect anything, but shit happens. Where is River? Why is she not here? She was part of all this."

"I have already talked with River, but if you want her here, then so be it." River appears next to me.

She says, "Hello, sweetie", like always. "Beverly, why am I here again? I thought we were good with things."

"We are, River, dear. Tigger wanted you here for support, I guess." Bev looks dead in my eyes. "Again, Paul. You are not here over what them fucking insects did."

"Then why?"

Bev once again picks up the paper. "The war of 1812, giving Einstein more than just a hand in things. Do you wanna hear more or are we both on the same page now?"

"I honestly either did not think there was any harm in what I did or I just didn't care. It doesn't matter what I say. The ball is in your court anyway with what happens from here on out." I am so tired of being here.

Beverly is pissed at this point. I am thinking I should not have pissed her off. "Fine. I was attempting to give you a way out of the mess you got yourself into. But if you don't care, then neither do I."

"Bev, wait! Looking back on everything that happened in that last life, I can understand why I am here. I want very much for you to understand that being in a life where Arron over there, who was my mother at the time, treated me like shit throughout my life was fucked up. She was the reason I did not care about shit. And a lot of the things I did in my 20's, I did just to spite her."

Beverly sits back in her chair and does not say a word for about five Earth minutes. The silence is deafening. Then someone enters with a note in their hand and gives it to Bev. I assume we are being observed but I have no clue by whom. She reads it and speaks.

"Okay, this is now out of my hands. It has been decided that you will return to when this all started. Damage control." I start to speak. "Shut up, I'm talking. Arron. You are to be his mother again but be warned, if you do him the way you did before, your ass is mine. I grow tired of this crap and I can only hope that we do not have to meet like this again." Bev allows me to stay in the room as she goes off on my mother-to-be again.

"And now to you, Arron Sun."

"What do you want me to say, Beverly? He hurt me."

Beverly stands up and so does Arron. Then Bev gets right in her face and goes off. "Do you remember your invisible friend, Tigger? Unknown to you, Arron, we had someone attached to Paul who watched every little thing he did and reported it back to us. We know it all! I haven't been this disappointed in anyone in a long time." I know better than to open my mouth. "Paul did not do what you said he did and we now have a record of the event. I think I will replay it for you."

I am then sent out of the room.

Present day

Here we go again. I am back in the womb, and I have done everything in my power to make Arron, or I should say, Cindy miscarry me. I would learn later that she was under strict bed rest for 3 months before giving birth. Everything I tried to get someone to kill me did not work as a child and the warning that was given to Arron did not seem to matter. She still treated me like shit.

Things went the way they did the previous time throughout my childhood, but it was not entirely the same. Everyone I ever had anything to do with back then seemed to remember their past life going through this all. I tried to use this to my advantage but most of the time it did not work. And I remembered my sweet Artemys. Oh, how I remembered her. Every fucking day of my life I remembered what happened when she was killed by that boy. It haunts me to this day and it's a wonder I am not nuts from it.

Now here is the interesting thing about Artemys you don't know and my so-called family could not do a thing about. I used to tell Art the horror stories about when I lived in the children's home in Maumee. So in 1970, Artemys got on the board for the home and was responsible for all the changes there in the early '70s.

The wall surrounding the home was taken down because of her and all the tunnels below the entire place were closed. The kids went to Maumee public schools, stopping a lot of the stuff taking place because the kids ran their mouths about it. Like the molestation going on there, though no one was fired over anything. They were put in positions where they could no longer be in direct contact with the children.

However, rumors went around about the bones surrounding the old intake building that was also a hospital. The house parents would rape the teenage girls and get them pregnant. Then right after birth, the babies would be killed and the children were buried outside of the building. This was confirmed, sort of, when they redeveloped the land a few years ago and dug up all the bodies. The news never did say why the bodies were there but all the kids that were there remembered.

The tunnels were closed until I came around and opened them back up. We found a doctor's office down there with a dentist's chair in it. That place was very creepy, and no one went in there except on a dare.

When I was 16, I was in the main building where all the offices were and where the kids would get their supervised visitation with their families. Artemys decided to look me up and things forever changed. She helped me fill in the blanks on a lot of things. I also kept my mouth shut and told no one about this because I knew that somehow my mother would fuck things up for me again. I would not see Art again for a long time after that day.

Now back to what I was talking about.

This puts a big twist in things that I am about to mention and to this day I do not understand it. This is the part that I think about every day, even though I know how events played out. In my 20's, Ohio Bell was on the ground floor of the Commodore. You could pay your phone bill there, get new phone service or get a new phone. I walked in one day in the winter time to get out of the cold. Never before had I been in the building in this timeline. As I went to walk past the stairs going up to the closed second floor restaurant, I was stopped by Artemys. A full body apparition of her. She asked me if I had seen her daddy. I get a big old smile on my face.

"Have I seen your daddy? Artemys, I am your daddy." We went back and forth in conversation for a few minutes before she ran back up through the blocked stairway and disappeared. She did not believe me. I have never forgotten this day and have it burned into my head.

Also, in my 20's, I was walking past Collingwood, which in this time is called the Collingwood Art Center. As I walk past, I see a kid climbing on the roof on the front of the building. I thought there were still Nuns that lived there since it was owned by the catholic church at this time. So, I told him to get down before he got hurt.

"I told you that you were not coming back for us," the kid said to me.

"Matthew. I remember you now. Ya, I am sorry about that. I died."

"I don't care. You lied to us."

Then the girl that used to sneak them all food comes half way out of one of the windows. "Matthew. Get inside before someone sees you. Oh, hi Doctor."

"Hi," I said and they both went back inside.

I then walked to the front door and banged on it til a Nun came and opened the door. "Hi, Doctor. It has been a long time. Nice to see you."

I then told her about the kids. She said there were no children there, then goodbye and closed the door.

When I got to my friend's house down the street, he told me that there hadn't been any Nuns living there in at least 10 years. This has never left my head, either, and sort of fucked me up, too, for a while.

The last thing about Art I am going to mention here is when I was like thirty-five, I finally had the balls to show up on Artemys' doorstep. I was with River for this. She lived in one of them big mansions along the Maumee river and I rode up on my Yamaha. She and her family came out to greet me and River.

Everyone was so nice to us. They invited us into their home and we all spent hours and hours talking. I think that the family was grateful to finally meet the woman who finished raising Artemys. I was not so sure they were happy about my presence.

I never went back. This ended up, to me, too much of a mind fuck. But River did several times and went to Art's funeral, as well. I did not go. I thought it was best since I was never a part of Artemys' life, that I should just stay away. I wish I had gone now, though. On with the story.

Now, I am going to jump up a bit since there is no reason to go all through my timeline again. Like I said, things are not exactly the same as before. For one, I lived with River in the 90's and we were not lovers this time. We did the cult movie thing again, but this time it was in the late 90's and not at the same time as when I was to be with Lynn. River and I talked about the previous life several times and she said she was not doing that again. She could not take the pain involved in that life. A lot of events did not correspond with one another anymore. 9/11, both towers came down this time instead of one. Oh, they made more than three Star Wars movies this time. The school shootings happened one after another in the past timeline and this time were spread over years. This makes it hard to predict things and work around them.

Something else different this time, I became one of the first pioneers in Internet radio. I was still into the Occult but not in a coven this time. I was too sick of life and more of a recluse, or a hermit. I didn't like to be around people and stayed to myself, mostly because I know how devious people are and I want nothing to do with them.

Let's skip ahead to my time with Lynn. This time we live together. We have been together now for over 15 years and things are not the same this time, either. My sister has never shown up and I haven't killed anyone, which was the whole reason I left this time in the first place. Artemys is back in my life, however, and my entire existence now is for her. Life has no other point to it anymore. I am hoping that things are different enough now, though, that things do not end the same way as before. Covid-19 is here in the timeline yet again. Artemys is almost at that age where she and everyone else die from CV or the Vaccine. Oh, and that is different, too. In the past timeline, there was only one vaccine and now they say they have a few. So I live through life day by day, using my magic to try to keep everything going smoothly.

For a few years, I did a paranormal podcast. Once a year, an event is held in September. A lot of ghost hunters attend to give speeches to people about hauntings and so forth. Ghost hunts are offered there, as well, since the building is said to be the most haunted building in Toledo. I have gone there with the hope that I might see the children again but the experience with them has never occurred again.

This time, I officiated both Lynn's son's and daughter's weddings. Lynn's daughter is not with the guy she was before when the Covid-19 shit happened. In fact, Lynn's daughter's stepchildren are the reincarnations of the kids me and River would talk to at Collingwood. Figure that one out.

One more thing about Artemys. Even though she is with me again in this life, the past life still haunts me to no end. It is something I have to get over, I suppose. But I still throw it around in my head that if something ever happens to Art, I will go back to 1960 and get her back.

Now, back to the present where myself, Will and River are sitting around the firepit. It's now dark and the fire makes everything around it look cool and eerie. I take a seat and relax a bit. Then River breaks her silence and speaks. "You know, Tigger. You forgot to mention that our Artemys is the reason you kept getting your bike back."

"Ya, I didn't think that was important, but okay. She always did keep an eye on me throughout the years and I knew it."

"You know, she really did miss you a lot. Always talked about you when I was around. I know she missed you but she did understand why you stayed away." River gets up and grabs the last of the scotch, taking a big swig. "Ugh. Now I remember why I hate this shit," she says while coughing her ass off and I start to laugh.

"Any questions, Will?" He just sits there, silent for about another ten minutes before he finally replies.

"Your mother only told me a small part of this story and I still find it hard to believe. Since I have now heard a lot of this stuff from several people, I suppose it can be true. Thank you for accepting me here tonight and telling me all of this."

"You are most welcome." About this time several people start to find their way to the firepit. I was not aware that River had asked people to stay away until I was done. They instead filled their time by playing a board game until I was finished.

I now take a break from my story telling for a few minutes to welcome everyone to the firepit. As people gather around the area, I tell them that I am in the middle of something but things will free up soon enough so that everyone can do what they want and talk about whatever. Since this next part of the story just happened, no one has heard this part of the tale til now, so this could get interesting.

"William, I am going to ask you to stick around just a bit longer, if you would. I am not done here yet and since no one has heard this until now, except River, this could get interesting."

"Okay, Tigger. I can do that. I have all night." Will says before asking someone for a beer.

River speaks up. She has been silent all night. This is not like her, so I make sure she can be heard. "While you have been talking, Tigger, I have been texting with Chris about what you are going to talk about. I wanted to see if he wanted to join us and add some more to the story."

"That is cool, River. Is he coming?"

"Yep, he should be here about now." River gets up and plays with the fire some.

Someone let the dogs out into the other part of the yard and they are going off. I see the headlights of a car pulling up into the drive and I know it is Chris. Since he has been here once before, I don't need to have anyone greet him and River tells him to come back to the pit.

As he walks to the pit I make sure he has somewhere to sit. Chris is the head of the paranormal team, The Paranormal Express, the leading ghost hunting team in the area where we all live.

I introduce Chris to everyone and give him a beer. "Thank you Tigger. You have quite a crowd here tonight. I thought you wanted to keep this all quiet."

"We are all family here tonight, so it is okay, I think, and most know the story except this part of it. I am glad you are here. This guy over here is my step-dad. He just heard the entire story tonight. He is a non-believer, as well, so let's see if we can change that."

Chris repositions himself on the big tree stump he is sitting on then speaks. "Okay, so who is going to tell this?"

"I am but feel free to jump in when you have stuff to add."

"Will do."

"As you all know, after years of trying to get Chris here to get me back into the Commodore Perry, he finally agreed to it. He did not want to believe that me and River knew who the ghost girl was but I think he does now. Don't ya, Chris? Oh, and just why did you finally give in? I never did ask you that."

"While I was with the owners of the building, I mentioned The Doctor and their eyes lit up. It was unbelievable. They said you are who you say you are and that I should take you in the building."

"Did they? Good to know someone remembers. It seemed as though everyone forgot. Okay anyway..." I begin.

Not one person on the team believed a single word of what I had told them. I think they did this just to humor me. Chris speaks up and agrees. As we were in the side street between the Secor Hotel and the Commodore. I heard, and I have always heard this, when I walk by the place. I heard "Daddy". Only one word but I heard it.

So I and Chris pulled our phones out and began recording so we could see if we could pick this up as an EVP since no one else heard this but me. Surprisingly, we got our first EVP but the team dismissed it as an EVP because it was outside. That was fine, I could accept this. The team has to have standards so they can stay credible.

So we all headed through the front door of the building and were greeted by security. They have their office in the center of the building, past the blocked off stairs to the restaurant. This is where I asked them to set up as a home base for the hunt tonight. I thought this was the best place because it would not bother any of the residents and because it would put some traffic downstairs. The ghost showed up when there were people around, or so it was said.

After the security guard told us what we were and were not allowed to do, we started to set up and got ready to go upstairs to the restaurant. Cathy and River were at the entrance talking. Then they heard someone say, "Have you seen my daddy?" The girls were both idly looking around but spun around when they heard this.

The girls then got all excited. To their amazement there was a girl, looking to be a young teenager, sitting on the steps of the restaurant. This was a full body apparition they were looking at. She had black hair and was wearing a white dress. River recognized the girl and while River struck up a conversation with her, Cathy turned on the recorder and set it on the step. Then she ran over to the hall and waved us all over to the entrance. Chris pulled out his video camera and started to record while trying not to be noticed.

I walked up and stood next to River. I spoke while trying not to cry. It was Artemys. "I am here, Sweet Pea." I crouched down so I could be non-threatening but still look Artemys in the eye. "I was hoping I would find you here."

Meanwhile, one of the team fired up the thermal camera and stood next to Chris. They both just stood silently with their jaws hanging open. Chris said under his breath that he had to pee but he wasn't moving.

Artemys asked me if I had seen her daddy. "Sweetheart, has it been that long you do not recognize us? This is River and I am your daddy." I said this as calmly as I possibly could because I was so afraid she would run off or simply disappear.

Artemys then had an attitude change. She smiled a bit then said, "My Pauly?"

"Yes, baby girl."

She did not talk to River at first. "You left me here!" She then got mad. "Why did you leave me here?"

River spoke up. "We left you with your friend's dad."

"He kicked me out. I have been waiting for you ever since." She was still mad.

Everyone was transfixed on what was going on. Even the security guard who was recording with his cell phone. No one could believe what they were witnessing. It was like watching a scene out of a movie, a once in a lifetime event.

I reached my hand out towards Artemys hoping she would take it, if possible. "Honey, you can come with me and River. We can go home now. Would you like to see grandma? I know you miss her."

"Don't touch me." Artemys was still mad, ignoring everyone else in the room but River and myself. "You left me here. Tell me what happened. Where did you two go?"

Me and River both looked at each other like "What the fuck?" It dawned on both of us that she did not remember things that she should and that this was only an aspect of Artemys. The part of her that stayed here after she died. The events of the past must have been so much more traumatic than either of us had realized.

"Artemys, I am sorry." I had to stop talking because I was almost in tears.

River asked, "Honey, can I have a hug? I missed the shit out of you."

Artemys stood up and began to come the rest of the way down the stairs to give River a hug. As they began to touch, Artemys disappeared and we both broke down in tears. Well, it was more like sobbing.

Through my crying, I heard someone say, "Did you guys get that? This is unbelievable!" I heard Chris say he did not get much 'cause his batteries kept dying and the security guy said his phone died.

A few minutes later, we all agreed it was time to go. So we packed up and left the building. The team was all amped up and excited. For them, I think it was confirmation of the existence of the other side. For me and River, it was another reason to live with guilt over past life events.

As me and River got on my bike to come here to the house, I heard "Daddy" again, only River heard it this time, too. I fired up the bike as fast as I could so that the sound of the pipes would drown out Artemys because I couldn't take any more.

I don't normally drink beer, but I need one after telling people about this event, so I grab one out of the cooler. Chris then speaks up.

"This was fucking amazing for me. All the batteries on all of our equipment kept dying and when we went back to look at what we did record, the girl did not show up except on the thermal camera. But we did get most of the conversation you guys had on EVP. No one will believe this is real. You just had to be there."

"That is one of the reasons I do not want this to be released, Chris. I do not want to make this into a spectacle. It is too personal. I also know that the owners of the Commodore do not want attention drawn to the place in this way." I light a cigar and finally take a seat.

"You know Tigger. I always thought you were full of shit about this story you would tell me. I am sorry for that. We should have done this sooner."

"It's okay, Chris, most people would think the same thing."

I didn't notice that River was crying over the last part of the story. As she wipes away her tears, she begins to talk. "I didn't tell you this before, Tigger. But I actually felt Artemys touch me for a second before she disappeared. That, I don't know if I will ever get over."

"I don't think I will get over this event either, River." I then take the last swig of my beer.

Now some interesting facts about the buildings I have talked about in this story that you can look up online.

The Commodore Perry: A memorable part of the Toledo skyline that has earned its spot in the pantheon of northwest Ohio folklore. Built in 1927, this historic, 19 story high-rise was, at one time, the center of luxury and glamour. The Commodore Perry Hotel is known for its lavish style and was host to many celebrities over the course of its history, Harry Truman, Bob Hope, Elvis Presley, Jimmy Stewart, and other notables.

Changing times and economic realities led to a re-imagining of the hotel and, in 1968, it re-opened as the Commodore Perry Motor Inn and operated until 1980 then became the Commodore Perry Apartments. These days, the Commodore Perry building is a luxury apartment home community with stunning views of the downtown Toledo area. The elegant style and the craftsmanship of its early days when it was a hotel have been restored and preserved for today's generation.

A few other things have remained as well. As the story goes, above the apartment areas in the building, there is an old, unused dance room and restaurant. It has been claimed that the ghost of a young girl, wearing a white dress, has been seen in these areas, as well as wandering the upper floors, or she sits at the bottom of the restaurant stairs. Many have claimed to have seen her sitting on the steps leading to the bar area in the restaurant. Inside this bar area is also an old piano that some claim to have heard playing all by itself.

The Oliver House: On a haunted note, The Oliver House served as a medical center for the wounded during the Spanish-American War and this historic hotel has a haunted reputation. Numerous apparitions have appeared to guests and diners over the years. The most common is that of a soldier who has come to be known as The Captain. He is said to show up most frequently dressed in full uniform. Paranormal investigations and strange sightings are common here. There are also rumors that Lincoln stayed there overnight.

The Collingwood Arts Center: The Collingwood Arts Center is a former convent for the Ursuline Order of the Sacred Heart, and later housed the Mary Manse College and St. Ursula Academy. It is a registered historical site. Since 1985, The Collingwood Arts Center has provided an outlet for creative involvement for the community while preserving an historic space. The structure was completed and ready for occupancy on September 6, 1905.

About the Author

Paul Ieson is a fascinating person. If you pay attention, you can see traces of The Magician from the Tarot cards. Science, music, experimentation and passion for life all coexist in dynamic balance. His writing is designed for fast reading while having a great time but the characters show ancient wisdom and the underlying world structure comes right from the arcane world. This can only be achieved by a writer who blends himself with the energy of youth, the wisdom of life, and a deep knowledge of how things really work.

Paul has been a songwriter, vocalist/musician for many years. He is an Ordained Minister and also enjoys woodworking. He holds an associate degree in Electronics and a degree in Physics. Paul lives in Millbury, Ohio at the moment and Paul's interests are studies in writing, music and he loves to travel.

Made in the USA
Columbia, SC
09 June 2024

36370551R10083